ROSARIO'S REVENGE

A San Juan Islands Mystery

(A Kindle Press series)

Book #4

The Writer
Dark Waters
Murder on Matia
Rosario's Revenge

D.W. Ulsterman

This is a work of fiction

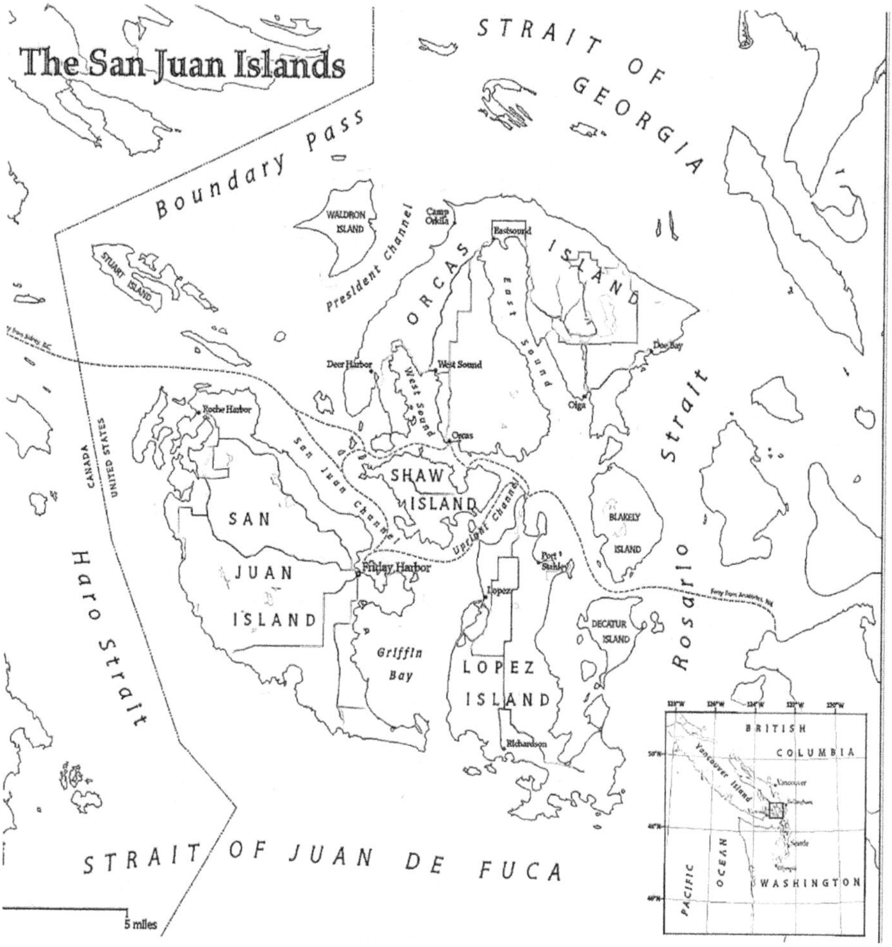
The San Juan Islands
STRAIT OF GEORGIA
Boundary Pass
WALDRON ISLAND
Camp Orkila
President Channel
STUART ISLAND
ORCAS ISLAND
Eastsound
East Sound
Doe Bay
Deer Harbor
West Sound
West Sound
Olga
Orcas
Roche Harbor
CANADA
UNITED STATES
San Juan Channel
SHAW ISLAND
Upright Channel
Rosario Strait
BLAKELY ISLAND
SAN JUAN ISLAND
Friday Harbor
Port Stanley
Lopez
DECATUR ISLAND
Haro Strait
Griffin Bay
LOPEZ ISLAND
Richardson
STRAIT OF JUAN DE FUCA
5 miles
BRITISH COLUMBIA
Vancouver Island
Vancouver
Seattle
PACIFIC OCEAN
WASHINGTON

Prologue

Sheriff Lucas Pine had never killed anyone before. Sergei Kozlov was determined to change that.

Lucas fired. One side of Sergei's head erupted in a red-mist cloud of blood and bone. The Russian didn't seem to realize he was already dead. His eyes blinked rapidly as he took a half-step back and his knees buckled. Sergei toppled face-first onto the asphalt with a wet thud. It was a horrible sound. Lucas looked away, wanting to throw up. Business owners peered wide-eyed through store-front windows. They had no doubt heard the shouting, the threats, and the sheriff's demand that Sergei drop his weapon followed by the single gunshot that ended Sergei's life.

It was early summer in the San Juan Islands. The Friday Harbor streets would soon be filled with the annual chaos of the peak season. Blood oozed toward Lucas's shoe. He shuffled backward as an arriving ferry blasted its horn. A growing throng of island residents and tourists now watched him. He still held his gun.

"Sheriff, are you OK?"

Lucas quickly holstered his weapon, took a deep breath, and lied. "Yeah, I'm fine."

He wasn't fine. His hands shook. He felt weak and cold. It was hard to move. Lucas crouched down and placed two fingers against Sergei's neck.

No pulse. Hearts don't normally beat for a man with half his head shot off.

The ferry's horn sounded again.

"You want me to go get help?"

Lucas closed his eyes and stood up. He was in the middle of the street two hundred paces from the ferry terminal – the heart of Friday Harbor's business district. His SUV was parked behind him with the motor still running. It was a cloudless, sunny morning, and unusually warm for this time of year.

"Sheriff?"

Lucas glanced at the older woman speaking to him. He finally recalled her name.

"Please step back, Ms. Hunt. Do you have a blanket I could use?"

Gladys Hunt scurried toward the front door of her San Juan Islands Whale Watching Tours business, repeatedly promising the sheriff she would be right back. As he walked to his vehicle to retrieve his phone, Lucas ignored everyone who watched. He saw them pointing and heard their whispers.

Lucas called his office. Samantha Boyler, who handled both reception and dispatch duties for the Sheriff's Department, answered on the second ring. Lucas quickly explained the situation. Samantha's tone made clear her concern for the sheriff's well-being. She promised to have the department's two deputies on the scene as soon as possible. She would also notify the coroner's office and contact the ferry terminal staff and instruct them to divert traffic away from the business district. Lucas thanked Samantha for her help, assured her he was fine, and ended the call.

The shaking in his hands had lessened but had been replaced by a headache. He heard footsteps and turned to find Gladys holding a blanket. Her eyes darted from side to side, looking everywhere but into his.

These people will never see me the same again.

"Here you go, Sheriff."

Lucas stepped forward. "Thank you."

Gladys dropped the blanket into the sheriff's hands, nervously pushed her glasses higher on her nose, and then made a hasty retreat to the sidewalk. Lucas walked slowly to where Sergei's body lay. He stared down at it and wondered why the Russian had confronted him in broad daylight in the middle of the busiest street on the islands with a gun drawn, screaming that Lucas was finally going to get what was coming to him.

It didn't make sense. Sergei was a petty criminal prone to acts of intimidation but had never been so stupid. It had been suicidal.

As Lucas covered the body, a ray of sunlight hit the metallic tip of Sergei's gun. Lucas bent down and used the corner of the blanket to pick it up. He was careful not to get his fingerprints on what was now a critical piece of evidence. It felt light - too light.

The gun was empty.

What the hell?

Lucas returned the weapon to its place near the body and stood up. It felt as if the entire town of Friday Harbor had already condemned him for the dead body in the street.

I didn't know the gun wasn't loaded. How could I? He pointed it right at me. I had no choice.

Lucas saw a second-story window with a "Lucas Pine for Sheriff" sign in it. The election was less than six months away. Sergei's death would require an inquiry from an outside law enforcement agency and generate considerable attention from regional media. In addition to the normal bustle of the tourist season, there would be the added complication of a Hollywood film crew that was to begin preparations for a movie based on the life of local author Decklan Stone. The director, Vincent Weber, was due to fly into Friday Harbor in just a few days. Lucas had already promised he would be there to greet Weber upon his arrival.

The summer would be a mess.

Lucas was suddenly very tired. The gun that hung off his hip felt unusually heavy from the weight of guilt and uncertainty.

I killed a man.

Lucas tried to convince himself it was all a terrible nightmare. Something he could wake up from. Only when he looked at the lifeless lump in the street was he forced to admit it was no dream. He had pulled the trigger and Sergei Kozlov was now dead.

A large seagull dropped from the sky and came to rest a few feet from the pool of blood that continued to seep out from beneath the blanket. The bird's head bobbed up and down as it inched closer to the body.

"Get out of here!" Lucas growled. The seagull took two sideways hops and then flew off. Vehicles continued to exit the ferry and were diverted by ferry staff away from the shooting scene. Lucas took a deep breath, let it out, and straightened his wide shoulders.

He had a job to do.

"Was this your first?"

Lucas looked up. A heavy-set, middle-aged man was staring back at him. He had a head of short, thick gray hair parted to the side. His fleshy face was clean-shaved. The sleeves of his dress shirt were rolled up over a pair of large forearms.

"Sir, I need you to step away. Please stay on the sidewalk."

Although the man smiled, his dark eyes remained hard. He held up both hands in front of him.

"I'm State Patrol. Or rather, I *was*. Retired last year. Just seeing if you needed any help with crowd control. Seems you're on your own, and there's a whole lot of traffic driving into town right now. My name is Dan Walser. I was on the job twenty-seven years. Saw my share of this kind of thing. It never gets easy. By the look on your face, I'd say my hunch was right. This *is* your first. Did he fire at you?"

Lucas's eyes narrowed. He shook his head.

"No."

Walser cleared his throat and arched a brow. "Ah, well, I'm sure you were justified in defending yourself. The victim was armed. I wouldn't worry."

Walser's words annoyed the hell out of Lucas. They had a hint of accusation in them. He didn't want the man's help, he just wanted him gone.

"Why would I worry? And why are you referring to the deceased as a victim?"

Walser took a step back. "No offense intended, Sheriff. I just know how these things work. There'll be lots of questions which have an unfortunate way of leading to allegations. Something like this happens, and pretty soon you have a bunch of outsiders poking around looking for wrongdoing. It's been my experience that if someone looks hard enough and long enough, they'll find something. Even the angels of heaven have blood on their hands. Did you know the victim prior to the shooting?"

Sirens went off in Lucas's head. He suspected it was no accident Walser had suddenly appeared on this particular morning under the guise of offering to help keep people off the street. That initial offer of help now felt more like an interrogation.

"Who are you?"

Walser cocked his head. "I told you, Sheriff. My name is Dan Walser. I was just stopping to see if a fellow lawman needed assistance. Is that a problem?"

Lucas's face tightened as his hand came to rest on the butt of his sidearm. "Why are you *really* here?"

Walser scowled and took another step back.

"Hey, you need to calm down. You don't want my help? That's fine by me. You take care, Sheriff Pine."

Walser spun around and started to walk away.

Lucas's headache grew worse along with the whispering and pointing from the crowd lining the street. At that moment, Lucas wanted nothing more than to run away. To hell with being sheriff, he just wanted to be left alone. He had awakened that morning to a job he loved. Killing someone had changed all that. It was a part of the job he had always known could happen but hoped never would. Whatever potential Sergei might have had, for better or worse, Lucas had permanently ended it. All that was left of him now was an empty shell.

Right before Walser disappeared into a sea of people, Lucas called out to him.

Walser turned and smiled. "What is it, Sheriff?"

Lucas kept his hand resting on his gun as he took three long strides toward the sidewalk. "I'd like you to come by my office later this afternoon."

Walser's smile widened even further. "And why is that?"

Lucas's jaw clenched. He was being toyed with.

"I might have a few questions I'd like to ask you."

Walser stepped back onto the street. The smile remained.

"I imagine you will, Sheriff Pine. The thing is, by then, you might find *you* are the one having to answer questions – not me."

Walser leaned forward and whispered his next words so only the two of them could hear. "Something doesn't feel right about this. I see it in your eyes. People *will* find out. Mr. Kozlov can't speak for himself anymore. You made certain of that, didn't you?"

Lucas's eyes narrowed as he wondered how Walser already knew Sergei's name. His hand tightened on his gun. Walser took a step back and nodded as his voice rang out.

"Absolutely, Sheriff, whatever I can do to help! It's like I said, we lawmen need to stick together. Of course I'll be at your office this afternoon. The people of these islands deserve no less. You have my word. I am at their service."

Walser disappeared into the crowd just as the ferry bellowed its low-pitched departure note. Lucas returned to his SUV to await his deputies. He tried in vain to push the image of Walser's smiling-smirk of a face from his mind. His world was about to be turned upside-down. He could feel it. Something bad was coming to the San Juan Islands.

For the first time in a very long time, Lucas Pine was afraid.

Chapter 1

Adele Plank wasn't happy to see Roland Soros leaving the islands. She didn't understand why he was doing so and Roland remained unwilling to explain. Whatever the real reason was, he seemed determined to keep it from her.

"You're just going to sail off into the sunset? What about the bank, all your business obligations?"

Roland grinned and shrugged. Adele knew he was trying hard to look nonchalant, but she detected the strain in his eyes. Something was bothering him.

"It's all taken care of. The vice president at the bank, Sandra Penny, will be handling all of my day-to-day operations. Don't worry. Your newspaper will still get a check every month for advertising."

Adele didn't care about the advertising and resented Roland suggesting she did. "This isn't about money, Roland. It's about *you*. Taking off like this – it doesn't make sense. Are you in some kind of trouble?"

Roland pretended to check his recently-purchased sailboat's dock ropes while Adele waited for him to answer. Finally, he stuck his hands into the back pockets of his shorts and leaned backward.

"I appreciate your concern, I really do. I just need some time away is all. Everything is fine." Roland pointed to the sailboat. "Hey, you haven't told me what you think."

Adele glanced at the vessel and nodded. It had been a few months since the Soros family yacht had been burned beyond repair while sitting in the very same Roche Harbor slip Roland's new sailboat now occupied.

"It's nice."

Roland ran his hand along the side of the boat's hull. "I actually won't use the sails much. I've never really had the patience for it. She's powered by a fifty-horsepower diesel outboard hidden under the stern cover. There's a large main tank and a reserve – five hundred gallons total. All customized to my specifications. Sips fuel. I can chug along at displacement speed for hours at a time and go a week before worrying about having to refuel. Two independent battery banks, a primary and backup generator, all commercial-rated navigation equipment; this thing is is the real deal. She'll take me anywhere I have to go."

Adele smiled at Roland's childlike enthusiasm for his latest toy. He caught her in the act and smiled back.

"What?" he asked.

Adele shook her head. "Nothing. I noticed you said this thing will take you where you *have* to go. Does that mean you don't want to leave? Is someone or something making you?"

Roland leaned against the boat and folded his arms across his chest. Several days of stubble covered the lower half of his deeply-tanned face.

"I don't like it when you play detective with me, Adele. Other than Sandra, you're the only one who knows I'm leaving. I invited you here because I *wanted* to. I figured you deserved to know I would be gone for a while."

Now it was Adele who folded her arms. "Why? Is it because we slept together? Does that make you feel obligated to keep me informed of your travel plans?"

A flash of annoyance crossed Roland's eyes. "I don't want to leave here arguing with you."

"When will you be back? And will I be able to get a hold of you while you're gone?"

Roland shrugged again. "If I need to contact you, I will. As for when I'll be back, that'll be when I'm ready and when it feels right."

"And you don't know when that will be?"

Roland shook his head. "No, I don't. I really wish I could give you more of an explanation, but I can't. It is what it is."

Adele scoffed. "It is what it is? *That's* what you want to call suddenly running away from your home, your business, and your friends? That's not a real answer, Roland. Something is wrong. I'm worried about you."

Roland's mouth opened, then closed, indicating he was about to say something but then thought better of it. Instead, he cleared his throat, paused, looked down at his feet, and frowned.

"How's Lucas holding up?"

It wasn't the first time someone had asked Adele that question since the shooting three days earlier. It seemed everyone on the islands was talking about it.

"I don't really know. He's been holed up inside his house since it happened. We've just spoken by phone a couple of times. He put himself on temporary leave pending the investigation. Last I heard, the State Patrol was on its way to begin interviewing witnesses. Lucas is a lot like you in that way. When something is bothering him, he bottles it up."

Roland winked. "And that annoys the hell out of you, doesn't it?"

Adele's lips pressed together. "Yeah, it does."

"Well, you tell Lucas I hope everything turns out OK. I know all about the sinking feeling that comes when outsiders start looking into how you conduct business."

Adele arched a brow. "What do you mean?"

Roland shook his head. "Nothing. I'm just a sympathetic supporter of our local sheriff, is all. We've had our differences, but he's a good man. I know that much. If he shot Sergei, he did so because he had to."

Adele wondered if Sergei's death and Roland's sudden and secretive departure were somehow connected given the two were former business associates. She was about to ask him when Roland cut her off.

"No, my leaving has nothing to do with Sergei."

Adele wasn't convinced. Sergei's history on the islands had been a brief but controversial one that directly involved Roland's attempt to develop a resort and casino atop the wind-swept grass fields of Cattle Point on the southern tip of San Juan Island. Sergei had acted as the go-between for Roland and Yuri Popov, a mysterious Vancouver B.C. businessman thought to be a boss in the Russian mob. Yuri's efforts to take over Roland's business interests were thwarted when Roland suddenly donated the entirety of his Cattle Point holdings to the county so the property could be used for a drug addiction treatment facility. Adele considered the possibility that Yuri blamed Sergei for Roland having temporarily gotten the better of him.

"Maybe it does, and maybe it doesn't. Either way, I don't think you would tell me. That doesn't mean I'm not going to look into it, though."

Roland's eyes narrowed. "Don't be messing with the likes of Yuri Popov, Adele. My business with him is finished. Sergei is dead. Yuri is back in Vancouver. Leave it at that."

Adele decided not to press Roland further on his true reasons for leaving. He clearly had no intention of telling her. If she wanted to get to the truth, she would have to find out on her own.

"I was hoping you'd be here for my birthday."

Roland's brows lifted as his mouth formed a circle. "Oh, that's right!"

He appeared to be genuinely disappointed.

"You won't be back by then?" Adele asked.

"I'm not sure. I wish I could promise I will be, but I can't," Roland answered.

Adele nodded. "OK, it's your choice. The invitation remains. You decide whether or not to accept it."

Roland wagged a finger. "I don't respond to guilt."

Adele stuck her chin out. "I wasn't trying to make you feel *guilty*, Roland. I was just reminding you that you still have a chance to do the right thing."

For the first time that morning, Roland tilted his head back and genuinely laughed. The sound made Adele realize how much she had missed hearing it. Then his laughter stopped. Each avoided the other's gaze until Roland held his arms out.

"I was hoping to get a hug from you before I go."

Adele didn't hesitate. Roland held onto her tightly. She did the same. Both knew the hug said far more than any words could about when Roland may or may not return to the islands.

Adele looked up. Roland looked down.

When he started to pull away, Adele placed her hands behind his neck, pulled him toward her, and kissed him lightly on the lips. He paused, grinned, and then kissed her back.

Soon after, Roland was on his sailboat and pulling away from the dock. Adele watched as he steered the vessel toward open water. She waited for him to turn around.

He finally did, with the palm of his hand extended out toward her. He sent her another smile. Their eyes locked. The smile collapsed. Roland turned his back on Adele. The sailboat became smaller and smaller until it disappeared into the horizon.

Adele wiped away a tear. There was very little wind. It was going to be another warm day. She stood looking down at the water for several minutes before walking toward the other side of the marina where she kept her own sailboat – a gift left to her two years earlier by a man named Delroy Hicks. Adele had met Delroy during her first summer in the San Juans. Delroy had died later that same year from cancer but not before leaving instructions in his will that his sailboat was to be given to Adele should she want it. She had accepted the gift and remained on the islands ever since.

"Excuse me, are you Adele Plank, the reporter for the *Island Gazette*?"

Adele stopped and turned around. She put a hand over her eyes to block out the bright morning sun. A stocky, gray-haired man stood a few feet from her.

"Yes. Do I know you?"

The stranger shook his head. "No, I don't believe you do."

Adele waited for him to say something more. He didn't.

"Can I help you?" she asked.

The man extended his hand and Adele shook it. His grip was strong. When she tried to break off the handshake, he squeezed more tightly, holding her in place.

"My name is Dan Walser. I was hoping to schedule a time when I could ask you a few questions."

Adele pulled her hand away. The name was vaguely familiar to her, but she didn't know why. What she did know is that whoever Dan Walser was, she didn't care for him.

"Questions regarding what, Mr. Walser?"

Dan smiled. It made him look like an overly content pig.

"The shooting incident the other day, the one between Sheriff Pine and Sergei Kozlov. I was told if someone wanted answers to things around here you were an excellent source."

Adele looked Walser up and down. "Who told you that?"

Walser took a deep breath. "I don't recall exactly. I've been speaking to a number of people the last few days. Have I done something to offend you? If so, I apologize. That was not my intent."

Adele's eyes narrowed. She suddenly recalled where she had heard the name before. Lucas had mentioned it to her the first time she had spoken to him after the shooting. Walser was the man who had offered to help keep the onlookers away from the body.

From across the marina, the sound of a yacht's twin diesel engines firing up caused the dock's wood planks to vibrate underneath Adele's feet. She gave Walser a tight-lipped frown.

"I'm a reporter, Mr. Walser, not an information service. If you wish to know what I think, read my articles like everybody else." Adele started to move away when Walser reached out and grabbed her by the arm.

"I find it curious you haven't written an article on the shooting yet. Why is that? Could it be you're trying to protect your friend the sheriff?"

Adele jerked her arm loose. "Don't put your hands on me! And you don't have any right to question me – about *anything*. I don't know why you're here on the islands or why you happened to show up right after the shooting, but I promise you I intend to find out."

An older male voice with a heavy Russian accent called out from behind Adele.

"Is everything as it should be?"

Adele found the phrase odd. Then, despite the warm sun, her skin went cold. She recognized the old man with the slicked back white hair dressed in the dark velvet track suit who stood leaning against a black cane She had seen him last winter as he was walking back from Roland's yacht - the same yacht that had been destroyed in a fire soon after. It was Yuri Popov.

Yuri glanced at Walser and then stared into Adele's eyes. She tried to look away but found she couldn't. Roland's recent warning echoed in her mind.

Don't be messing with the likes of Yuri Popov, Adele.

"Young lady, is this man bothering you?" Yuri asked, continuing to hold Adele's eyes hostage in his own.

Adele finally managed to look away. She shook her head.

"I'm fine. Thank you."

Yuri smiled and nodded. "That is good. You are such a pretty, smart thing. I would not wish to see one such as you bothered by strange men. These islands are beautiful, but as you already know, they can be dangerous as well."

Adele attempted to step away from Yuri but bumped up against Walser who had quietly positioned himself behind her. Yuri leaned forward, leering down at Adele close enough she could see the shades of yellow on his dentures.

"Tell me, have you seen our friend Roland lately?"

Walser's hands clamped down on Adele's shoulders with enough force that she cried out in pain.

"Gentlemen, step away from my friend."

Yuri squinted as he tried to make who had just issued the order. Adele, however, already knew who it was. She heard footsteps behind her. Walser's hands fell away as he turned around. Adele pushed past him and gave Tilda Ashland a grateful smile. The tall, red-haired owner of the Roche Harbor Hotel glanced at Adele.

"You alright?"

Adele nodded.

"Do you know these men?"

"The older one is Yuri Popov."

Tilda looked like she had just smelled something foul. "Ah, I see."

Yuri moved in front of Walser and scowled at Tilda. Tilda glared back, unblinking and without fear. They stood like that for several seconds. Adele hoped she wasn't witnessing an unspoken declaration of war between the two. Yuri pointed at Tilda and snarled.

"Mind your own business, old woman. Do you know who I am?"

Tilda stepped forward; she towered over both men.

"I don't care who you are, Mr. Popov. This is Roche Harbor. That means *you* are the one who should be worried about who *I* am."

Tilda put her arm around Adele's shoulders. "C'mon, let's go."

Adele felt the eyes of Yuri Popov and Dan Walser on her as she left. Tilda looked straight ahead as she whispered to Adele.

"I was watching from the hotel and saw them circling you. I arrived here as quickly as I could. Do you have any idea what the hell that was all about?"

Adele shook her head. "No, not really. Yuri was asking about Roland. He wanted to know where he was. The other one is Dan Walser. He was in Friday Harbor when Lucas shot Sergei."

Tilda's arm tightened around Adele. "And that would be the same Sergei who worked for Yuri Popov, correct?"

Adele nodded. "That's right."

Tilda's pace slowed as they neared the hotel. Adele knew that was the place her friend felt most safe. Tilda turned and looked down at the marina.

"I believe we are about to have an especially interesting summer."

Yuri Popov was still standing where they had left him, staring up at the hotel. Adele knew Tilda was right. Things were likely about to get very interesting – and dangerous.

Chapter 2

They were running late. Tilda urged Adele to drive faster. Vincent Weber was due to fly into the Friday Harbor airport very soon.

For Adele, having Tilda in the passenger seat of her MINI was a surreal experience. She had never seen Tilda beyond the borders of the Roche Harbor resort, let alone wearing blue jeans and tennis shoes.

"Stop looking at me."

Adele struggled to hide her grin. "I'm sorry. It's just a little weird seeing you out and about dressed like us common folk."

Tilda grunted. "Indeed."

"Where's Brixton?" Adele asked.

Brixton Bannister was the Hollywood actor the world believed had died several years ago after his plane was thought to have plunged into the waters surrounding the San Juan Islands. Tilda and Adele were among the few to know the truth. Brixton had actually retreated from all the trappings and burdens of fame while living in a cave on a large rock called Ripple Island a few miles north of Roche Harbor. The next Vincent Weber film was to be Brixton's return to his former life as an international movie star.

"He took a cab to the airport. He wanted to make certain he wasn't late."

Adele sped into a corner on the road between Roche Harbor and Friday Harbor. She was reminded of her first trip on that same road when she was the passenger in a car being driven by her friend Suzanne Blat, owner of the Friday Harbor bookstore. Back then, Adele had been amazed at how Suze drove so fast while hardly looking at the road, having driven it so many times before. Now it was Adele who was doing the same. In the space between those few years, she had truly become an islander.

"Are you worried about Brixton? Do you think he might not be able to handle all the pressure? It won't just be the movie, after all, it will be his return. He's supposed to be dead. The media attention on him is going to be pretty intense."

Tilda stared out the passenger window at the tall grass fields. Her eyes narrowed.

"Yes, it won't be easy for him, but he's convinced himself it's what he wants."

Adele took another tight turn. One of the MINI's front tires chirped.

"It's going be so different than all that time Brixton had to himself on Ripple Island. I worry about how it might mess with his head. He has always seemed like such a fragile man. And what about Decklan and Calista? I haven't heard from them either, which is a bit odd. It makes me wonder if they might be having second thoughts about all this, too."

The mystery of Decklan and Calista Stone had been the motivation for Adele's initial arrival to the islands. Like Brixton, Decklan had retreated from the world following what he thought was his wife's drowning. The shocking and remarkable story of Calista's survival set in motion what was now to be Vincent Weber's film, *The Writer*, the title of which was inspired by an article of that same name written by Adele shortly after Calista's rescue.

Tilda cleared her throat. "They wouldn't be the only ones."

Adele slowed down as she glanced at Tilda. "What? You think the film might be a mistake?"

Tilda closed her eyes and shook her head. "I don't know. Like I told you, it's what Brixton wants."

"You keep saying that – it's what *he* wants. What do *you* want Tilda?"

Tilda didn't answer; she was looking out at the passing fields again. Adele continued to slow down.

"Does Brixton know how much you care about him?"

Tilda scowled. "Of course he does."

Adele pulled the car over to the side of the road. "Look at me. This is important. I'm not talking about as friends or being a supporter of his career. Have you told Brixton how you *really* feel about him?"

"He cares for me, and we care for each other. We've been friends for some time. You know this, Adele. Don't attempt to make me explain the obvious."

Adele waited until Tilda turned to face her. "Then don't keep avoiding the obvious. If you have concerns about this movie being made, or how it might affect Brixton, you should tell him. And the same goes for your feelings. If you really care about him, then he should know that."

Tilda sighed. "It wouldn't be right to have my feelings influence what is best for him. Brixton wants to do this film. He wants to play the part of Decklan. He feels very deeply that his having spent so many years alone makes him perfect for the part. Who am I to try and stop him from doing so? And what if my concerns are nothing more than my own insecurity in knowing this film will return him to Hollywood? He'll be the man he was, not the one he has been with me since he allowed the world to think he was dead. I have no right to demand his life here is to be the only life for him. That choice should be his and his alone. Besides, he's too young for me."

Adele snorted through her nose. "Hah! Don't give me that. Brixton is what, ten years younger?"

Tilda smiled. She appeared to be warming to the conversation.

"You know, he looks like a schoolboy next to me since he shaved his beard."

Shaved was an understatement. Prior to cleaning himself up for his leading role in *The Writer*, Adele recalled Brixton looking and often smelling like a deranged island hermit. She wagged her finger.

"I don't buy your insecurity for a second. I doubt Brixton Bannister is the only one around these islands interested in getting to know your romantic side. Money and mystery are two potent aphrodisiacs and believe me, you have plenty of both."

Tilda lifted her head, arched a brow, and folded her arms across her ample chest. "I suppose you're right. I do remain a remarkable woman."

Adele laughed. "There's the aristocratic arrogance I've missed!"

Tilda's mood turned quickly back to melancholy reflection. "I've tried love, Adele. Be it with a man or a woman, it never seems to work out. In the end, I'm always left alone. Why would this be any different? I don't wish to sound as if I'm complaining. I'm not. I have a wonderful life now – one of my choosing, made all the better by friends like you. But love? No, I don't think it's for me. Experience suggests I should have the good sense to grow old gracefully free from the distractions of romance. I'm inclined to agree."

Adele's brow furrowed. "Stop feeling sorry for yourself, Tilda. If you really want a chance to be with Brixton, you should tell him. If he does end up leaving here without knowing, you're going to regret it. You know I'm right."

Tilda glanced down at the gold watch on her wrist. "We should get going. Why did you stop, anyway? You seem quite capable of talking and driving at the same time."

Adele pointed at something in the field. "I wanted to hear what Millie thought about all this."

Tilda turned her head and screamed. Adele had never heard Tilda cry out like that before and found it hilarious. Even Tilda's cold stare couldn't stop the giggles from coming.

Millie was the island's resident camel. She roamed a multi-acre roadside ranch and had become as big a tourist attraction over the years as the summer whale-watching tours. When a car stopped to get a better look at her, as they often did, she would make her way toward it, hoping for a snack. Her long furry neck would extend across the top of the barbed wire fence and bob up and down. If no snack was promptly given, the camel would let out a disappointed wail.

Tilda had no snack. Millie's mouth opened wide as she unleashed a long, frustrated groan and bumped the roof of the MINI with her chin. Tilda screamed again. Adele's giggle turned into tears-streaming-down-her-face laughter. She opened the glove box and withdrew a shiny green apple.

"Roll down the window."

Tilda was horrified. "*What?*"

"I stop and give Millie an apple all the time. Don't worry. She won't hurt you."

Adele placed the apple in Tilda's hand and motioned for Tilda to hurry up. Tilda gave the camel a worried look.

"We're going to be late. Just reach out and give it to her. She'll eat it right out of your hand, just like a horse."

Tilda's jaw tightened. "If you're trying to convince me, you're going about it all wrong. I've never fed a horse."

Millie's breath temporarily fogged up the outside of the passenger window. Her lips started to vibrate as if she was trying to make bubbles underwater.

"C'mon Tilda, she's waiting. Give her the apple. Then you'll have a new friend."

"Good. It'll make it easier to replace you after we're done here," Tilda growled. She rolled down the window and slowly extended her hand outside. "You promise she won't bite?"

Adele nodded. "I promise. Millie is a gentle old girl. You'll see."

Millie sniffed the apple and then carefully took it from Tilda's hand. Tilda's grimace softened into a faint smile as Millie began to chew the fruit. Adele wiped away the last of her laughing tears and put the car into gear. Before pulling away, she honked the horn.

"See you next time, Millie!"

The camel bobbed her head up and down as Adele sped off. They would arrive at the Friday Harbor airport in just a few minutes. Tilda shifted in her seat while looking out the window.

"Funny how having a camel take an apple out of my hand can remind me just how great a blessing it is to call these islands home. Is there any other place so unique, so ruggedly beautiful and filled with genuine people you can call real friends? I don't think so. Thank you for helping to remind me of this, Adele. I needed it."

Adele sped past the "Welcome to Friday Harbor" sign, and then downshifted to obey the city speed limit of thirty-five.

"Did I see you speaking with Roland Soros this morning?" Tilda asked. Adele suspected Tilda already knew the answer.

"Yeah, he bought a new boat – a sailboat."

Tilda had been there last winter when the Soros family yacht was destroyed by a fire some suspected had been ordered by Yuri Popov. Adele felt Tilda's eyes on her.

"Interesting that Yuri arrived in Roche Harbor so soon after your conversation with Roland. Might those two things be related?"

Adele wasn't sure if she was supposed to keep Roland's sudden departure for parts unknown a secret from others. She decided to say as little as possible by answering a question with one of her own.

"What do you mean?"

Tilda shrugged. "Oh, I don't know. It just seems odd that Roland would buy a new boat, meet with you, and then sail off right before Yuri arrives given all the history those two have. It looked to me as if Roland was running away. Is he in some kind of danger?"

Adele tried to hide her concern that Roland might really be in danger - the kind of danger that would keep him from ever returning to the islands. "I don't know. He didn't say."

"You should inform the sheriff that Yuri is on the islands," Tilda suggested. Adele nodded.

"Yeah, I will." She had already planned to do so.

It took a while to find a place to park; the airport was especially busy. Adele had to settle for a spot at the very back of the long gravel parking lot. The entrance to the outdoor arrival area was two hundred yards away. The sound of single-engine planes coming and going vibrated inside the MINI.

The afternoon air was warm and still. Tilda checked her watch again. "His plane should be arriving any minute. Should we go?"

Adele started to move toward the entrance. "Sure, right behind you." The two had taken just a few steps when a deep voice called out behind them.

"Hey, Adele – wait up."

Adele turned. Lucas Pine was walking toward her dressed in shorts and a t-shirt, his handsome square-jawed face covered in the beginnings of a beard. Adele smiled.

"You're looking rather casual today, Sheriff."

Lucas paused, looked down at his attire, and then shrugged. "I'm not the sheriff, remember? Just a guy on paid leave pending the conclusion of an investigation. It's summer in the San Juans. I figured I should take the opportunity to look the part."

Tilda tapped the top of her watch. "Sorry to cut short the reunion but the plane could be arriving."

Lucas extended his hand. "By all means, lead the way. God forbid we don't give Mr. Hollywood our full and undivided attention."

Tilda walked several paces ahead while Adele waited for Lucas to move next to her. She was surprised to find him in such good spirits.

"Word is you were sitting at home."

Lucas grunted. "I was. It was more a matter of staying out of the way. I didn't want to be accused of trying to influence the inquiry."

"Any idea when it will be over and you can get back to work?"

Lucas shook his head. "No, not really. A few weeks – maybe more. I haven't even had my psych evaluation yet."

Adele slowed her pace as she looked up. "Psych evaluation?"

Lucas nodded. "Yeah, it's nothing to worry about - standard procedure. After a shooting, there are some very clearly-defined steps that must be taken. I already handed over my weapon for the forensic work and had a blood test to make sure I wasn't under the influence of anything at the time of the shooting. Now the state is sending someone from Bellingham to interview me. They need to confirm I'm not suffering from depression, posttraumatic stress, that kind of thing. I mean, a man *did* die, and I was the one who shot him, right? It's basic due-diligence that I get checked out before I resume my duties."

Though Adele was relieved to see Lucas looking and sounding so relaxed, she also found it slightly unsettling. It didn't feel real. It wasn't him. She wondered how much of what he really thought was lurking just beneath the surface. He nudged her with his elbow.

"It'll be fine – really. I'm more worried about the election, actually. That and how much work it's been for poor Gunther and Chancee having to pick up the slack during my absence. Thank goodness we have someone coming in to be interim sheriff. He's supposed to start first thing Monday."

Gunther Fox and Chancee Smith were Lucas's two loyal deputies. Adele hadn't heard anything about a temporary sheriff, though, which bothered her given she was the reporter for the local newspaper. Knowing things before others did was her job. Lucas must have noticed Adele's confusion. He quickly tried to explain.

"Again, it's standard procedure. We want someone outside the department to help oversee the investigation. He's former State Patrol which makes him an appropriate liaison between my department and the state authorities during the inquiry. I don't know much about him beyond that."

Despite the summer temperature, Adele felt a chill run through her. She reached out and tugged on the back of Lucas's shirt. He stopped and turned around.

"What is it?" he asked.

Adele searched Lucas's eyes for any sign he was hiding something from her. "What's the name of the interim sheriff?"

Lucas frowned as he cocked his head. "Why?"

Tilda had already passed through the airport entrance gate. Either she hadn't noticed Adele and Lucas had stopped walking, or she didn't care. Adele looked up at Lucas and thought she might have seen a hint of real feeling. He wasn't OK. It wasn't standard procedure. He had shot and killed Sergei Kozlov, and that act was now haunting him.

"It's Dan Walser, isn't it? The same guy you mentioned earlier who showed up right after the shooting."

Lucas flinched. Finally, there was a visible crack in his facade. He betrayed the worry he was trying so hard to hide.

"How'd you know that? His position hasn't been announced to anyone outside the department or the county council, and I ordered both Chancee and Gunther to keep quiet."

Adele looked around, feeling as if someone was watching them. She decided to tell Lucas everything she knew about Dan Walser but to wait until after Vincent Weber's arrival at the airport.

"We need to talk, but this isn't the time or place. Can I come by your house tomorrow?"

Lucas shrugged. "Sure, no problem. Is it something serious?"

Adele's eyes scanned the parking lot. The feeling of being watched grew stronger. Though he was trying to hide it, Lucas's tone suggested he had already been worrying about Dan Walser's arrival to the islands as well. She nodded.

"Yeah, I think so."

Chapter 3

"I believe that's it." Tilda pointed to a twin-engine Cessna that had just landed and was taxiing down the island airport's single asphalt runway. Brixton stood with his hands clasped behind his back, biting down on his lower lip while he waited for Vincent Weber to appear.

Besides Adele, Tilda, Brixton, and Lucas, no one else knew about the Hollywood director's arrival. Not that it would have mattered much to the locals. The islands had long been a get-away-from-it-all destination for the rich and famous. From John Wayne to Steven Tyler, the San Juan Islands offered a remote and beautiful place to unwind among island residents who had the collective good manners to give their celebrity visitors some space.

Adele gasped when she saw the first person step off the plane. She jogged onto the tarmac with an ear-to-ear grin. Decklan Stone opened his arms and hugged her tight.

"It's so good to see you again, young lady."

Adele's eyes were wet with tears, but she didn't care. Calista stepped out from behind Decklan and hugged Adele as well.

"We hoped we might surprise you," Calista remarked.

Tilda came forward to embrace her old friends as Lucas introduced himself. Tilda then pointed to Brixton who had remained standing a few paces back.

"Decklan, this is Brixton. He is the one who'll be playing you in the film."

Decklan shook Brixton's hand and asked Calista what she thought of him. Calista looked Brixton up and down and then did the same to her husband. "I worry he's much too young and good-looking to be playing you, Decklan," she teased.

Decklan's eyes narrowed as he pretended to be offended. "Oh, is that right?"

Someone cleared their throat. Decklan and Calista moved to the side to reveal a young and very thin Asian man. His medium-length dark hair was pulled back from a lean, sharp-edged face that framed full lips covered in black gloss. He spoke in a soft voice that was difficult to hear.

"My name is Vincent. You must be Adele – the reporter. I enjoy your articles a great deal. I've read them all."

Vincent Weber was far more diminutive in person than his media pictures suggested. He was the same height as Adele but looked to be much lighter. Adele shook his hand. Vincent's grip was weak, the skin baby-soft. She could feel the birdlike bones in each of his fingers. He avoided looking directly at her. Instead, his eyes darted from side to side or down at his feet.

Tilda gently pulled Brixton toward her. "Mr. Weber, I'd like you to meet Brixton Bannister."

Vincent's eyes widened slightly. He looked up at Brixton, stared at him for a few seconds, and then looked away. He stepped toward Lucas. "I like your face and your body. You have real gravitas - a genuine man. Who are you?"

Lucas glanced at Adele. She shrugged. He extended a hand toward Vincent. "Uh, I'm Sheriff Lucas Pine."

Vincent stared at Lucas's hand.

"You're strong. You can't fake that kind of strength on film. Some try, but I *always* see how they are pretending. That kind of dishonesty disgusts me."

Vincent glanced at Brixton as he said "disgusting".

"I need a guide to help me scout locations, Sheriff. You can help provide the truth my films require. It shouldn't be more than a few weeks. I'll compensate you, of course. The studio is paying for everything. Name your price."

Again, Lucas looked at Adele, and again she shrugged. Vincent smiled and put a hand on Lucas's muscular forearm.

"I said name your price, Sheriff Pine. *Please.* I require the guidance of a good man. This project remains a long way from a true beginning. Many hurdles remain before filming begins."

Everyone watched the unusual spectacle of the sheriff being so easily intimidated by a man half his size. Adele fought back a smile as Lucas shook his head.

"I apologize, Mr. Weber. I have a lot on my plate right now."

Vincent's tiny shoulders slumped. "I'm sorry to hear that, Sheriff. If you should reconsider, don't hesitate to contact me.

I'll be staying at the Rosario Resort. I've seen the photos online; it looks remarkable. I intend to scout that location first."

Tilda frowned. "What? You're not staying at my hotel in Roche Harbor? I already prepared a room for you, Mr. Weber."

Vincent turned his head toward Tilda, saw her glaring at him, and quickly looked away.

"I don't recall my office telling any of you where I would be staying. If there is any confusion over that, it didn't come from me. Now, who will be driving me to Rosario?"

Lucas chuckled. "Rosario is on another island – Orcas Island. You don't drive there unless it's by boat."

Vincent's cheeks reddened slightly. "Of course, that's what I meant. So, who will be taking me? The sea is essential to the story. This will allow me the opportunity to experience it first-hand. Might it be you, Sheriff Pine?"

Lucas quickly shook his head. "No, no. I'm afraid I'm busy."

No one else in the group offered. Vincent put his hands on his hips and pouted. "Come now, *someone* here must be willing to deliver me safely to Rosario."

Each time Vincent mentioned Rosario, Tilda's jaw clenched. Brixton appeared to still be hurt by Vincent's rebuke. Decklan and Calista remained silent as well.

That left Adele. "I'll do it. I need to return Decklan's runabout to him."

Decklan shook his head. "Oh, that's all right, Adele. You're welcome to continue keeping it at your slip in Roche Harbor."

Adele knew better. Decklan would want his boat back. For residents of the San Juan Islands, a person's boat was often an extension of their soul – a required necessity to island life. She gave both him and Calista a warm smile.

"I don't mind. It'll give me a chance to stop by your home on my way back from Rosario."

Calista reached out and gave Adele's shoulder a gentle squeeze. "I'll prepare dinner and open a bottle of wine. You can stay the night and then Decklan can take you back to Roche Harbor in the morning."

Adele happily accepted the invitation. "That would be wonderful. Thank you."

Vincent clasped his hands together in front of him. "Good, then it's settled. Now, if you could please grab my bag from the airplane and tell me where your vehicle is parked?"

Adele caught Lucas smirking. Clearly, he was pleased to see Adele had replaced him as the focus of Vincent's attention. She pointed toward the parking lot.

"It's right through the gate, Mr. Weber – the blue MINI at the back."

Vincent walked quickly toward the gate without saying goodbye to the others. Tilda let out a disgusted sigh.

"What a disappointingly odd little man."

Calista nodded. "He is that. He hardly spoke during the flight from Seattle. Decklan tried to engage him, talk about the screenplay, but he just sat in his seat looking out the window the whole time. Frankly, I find him rude. Genius or not, I really don't care for him."

Tilda arched a brow. "That makes two of us." She turned to face Brixton. "This is *your* fault. You brought him here. And for what? We all watched how he treated you. I wouldn't be so upset right now if you had stood up for yourself. The old Brixton would have. The one who lived alone on his island would have throttled anyone who spoke to him like that."

Brixton grew smaller with each word Tilda flung at him. Adele did her best to ease the tension.

"It's fine, Tilda. He was just caught off guard by Mr. Weber. We all were. Heck, I was the one who agreed to take him to Rosario."

Tilda muttered "Rosario", took a deep breath, and then shook her head while looking at Decklan and Calista. "I'm sorry for my mood. I was so excited about the film and now…I can't stand the thought of that man directing your story. He isn't worthy of it! Enough of him, though. You're both back here where you belong. I would love to have you over to the hotel for a celebration. Something intimate, just a few of us. Perhaps this weekend?"

Calista wrapped her arm around Decklan's and nodded. "That would be wonderful, Tilda. Thank you. And, might I add, you're looking *very* well."

The shine in Tilda's eyes indicated how much the compliment pleased her. "As do the both of you. We're older, but it seems this particular batch of years suits us - at least for now."

The pilot, a bald, middle-aged man wearing sunglasses announced he was getting ready to move the plane back into its hangar and that everyone should make their way to the gate. His hand gripped the handle of a large suitcase. "This belongs to Mr. Weber," he said.

Adele stepped forward and took the suitcase and was immediately grateful it had wheels. It was very heavy. Before the pilot re-entered the plane, Tilda asked if he would use her phone to take a picture.

They all stood shoulder to shoulder as the pilot told everyone to smile. Adele looked down and found Calista holding her hand. The late afternoon sun's descent toward the watery horizon created long shadows that extended over the runway like fingers reaching out for the soon-to-be darkness.

Chapter 4

The water between Roche Harbor and Rosario was green-blue glass. The runabout skimmed across the surface at top speed, its outboard engine growling a happy tune.

Vincent Weber's knuckles were white and his face the color of pale peas. Despite the smooth ride, he still managed to become seasick. Adele attempted to take his mind off his discomfort by pointing to tree-covered shoreline they were passing.

"That's Jones Island. If you look closely, you might spot some black-tailed deer walking along the beach."

Though deer were found throughout the San Juan Islands, they were most prevalent on Jones Island where they lived free from predators and fed from the two-hundred acres of abundant thick mossy grass and fruit trees that covered the island's interior. Humans weren't the only ones who found the San Juans the perfect place to live.

"There's some deer coming out of the woods now!" Adele shouted.

Vincent barely looked up. Despite his earlier claim that he wanted to experience first-hand what it was like to travel from island to island by boat, he now appeared entirely focused on not throwing up. Adele decided to ignore his condition. It was early evening – her favorite time to be on the water. In the sky were several great blue herons flying to their nests for the night. Their wings were silhouetted by the setting sun's gold-flecked light. On Adele's right was an assortment of large, dark rocks that broke apart the water's surface – the Wasp Islands. Over the years, they had gouged holes into the hulls of many a boat piloted by captains unfamiliar with the area and the dangers it posed, particularly at low tide. Adele had come to know them well. She deftly steered the runabout between the rocks and was soon blasting through the middle of Wasp Passage on her way to Rosario.

It took just over twenty minutes for Adele to see the unmistakable sea-green copper roof and white arches of Rosario Resort rising from the cliffs overlooking East Sound. The water remained calm all the way. Longtime island locals knew the resort as the Moran Mansion, originally constructed by Seattle mayor and shipbuilder Robert Moran. Moran had moved from Seattle to Orcas Island after being told by his doctor in 1905 that he had just one year to live. He died forty years later, having outlived both his wife and his doctor. The 25,000-square-foot mansion was later transformed by new owners into an elegant seaside resort destination that offered guests a marina, restaurant, lounge, and spa. Where San Juan Island's Roche Harbor was rustic chic, Orcas Island's Rosario remained undeniably high-class – a location that would be right at home in a scene from a James Bond film. Yet, despite its posh trappings, those in the know regularly traveled to the resort to enjoy something simple: the world's most mouth-watering burger and fries.

When Adele suggested the local favorite to Vincent after tying up the boat at the resort's guest dock, he grimaced. "Meat? Are you insane?"

Adele could care less about Vincent's eating habits. She needed to get going. With a loud grunt, she dropped his suitcase onto the dock and then instructed him to follow the trail up to the mansion. He stared back at her like a child who had lost his parents.

"You're not going to make sure I return safely to my room?"

Adele was already untying from the dock. "No. I have about fifteen minutes of light left to get to Deer Harbor. You'll be fine, Mr. Weber. The staff here will get you whatever you need. If you think you would like someone to show you around tomorrow, I'm sure Brixton would be happy to help. He knows the islands as well as anyone."

Hearing Brixton's name made Vincent appear as if he bitten into something sour. "You mean the lost celebrity who calls himself an actor? No thanks."

Adele wanted to put in a good word for Brixton but was running out of time. She didn't like to be on the water at night.

"Got to go," she said right before pulling away from the dock and then speeding off toward Deer Harbor.

Adele pushed the throttle forward. She inhaled the sea-salt air as it struck her face, happy to be alone on the water. By the time she zipped through the narrow and shallow southern entryway into Deer Harbor called Pole Pass, it was dark. Adele had to strain her eyes to see the rock and trees outline of Decklan's private island home. She couldn't help but be reminded of her first trip to that same island when she was still a journalism student in college. It had just been a few years earlier but felt like a lifetime ago.

So much had changed.

The islands remained the same, however. Decklan and Calista were back home where they belonged.

The runabout bumped against the dock. Adele cut the engine and tied off. Footsteps approached. She looked up to see a light bouncing toward her.

"Calista was worried. I promised her I'd be here to greet you when you arrived. I watched you come in; you're a natural on the water now, Adele. Quite an improvement from when we first met."

Adele hopped onto the dock and stretched. "Thanks," she said. She looked down at the runabout. Decklan stood next to her.

"I'm still willing to let you keep the boat at your slip in Roche Harbor."

Adele shook her head. "No, it's time I buy one for myself. I already have a few in mind."

Decklan's gaze went from Adele to the boat and then back to Adele. He nodded once and put his hand around her shoulder.

"If you change your mind, the offer stands. Now, we better get going. Calista has dinner ready. She's pretty excited to be cooking in her own kitchen again."

Adele followed Decklan up the hillside trail that led from the dock to the house. When they arrived at the clearing at the top of the hill, he paused. The big home was lit up from inside. Adele spied Decklan looking at it.

"It's a home again – alive and welcoming. Calista and I spent the last couple of years going everywhere and anywhere we wanted. We saw her family back in New York, then it was off to Europe, Asia, North Africa, and we even spent a few weeks walking the beaches of New Zealand but none of it, as beautiful as it all was, compares to the feeling of being back here with Calista and seeing you again."

Decklan turned and stared across the water at the lights of the Deer Harbor Marina. The sky was filled with a million blinking stars. What little breeze there was carried the scent of dry pine needles and the sea.

"From the moment you crossed the water from Deer Harbor to come to this island, everything I have with Calista, everything I will *ever* have, I owe to you, Adele. You helped bring us both back from the dead. You returned our lives to us. It's a debt I could never hope to repay, but I'll do my best to try."

The sound of seals frolicking in the nighttime water filtered through the island trees. It was a common occurrence during the San Juan summers as male seals tried to earn the attention of their female counterparts by loudly slapping the surface with their fins. The savory aroma of Calista's cooking drifted from the house, swirled around Adele, and made her stomach growl. Decklan chuckled.

"I'd say that's a signal it's definitely time to eat."

It was a remarkable meal. Not so much due to the food, but because of the quality of the company. Adele, Decklan, and Calista talked as if no time had passed between them. They told her of their many trips, used their phones to show her pictures, drank some wine, laughed at jokes both given and received, and drank some more.

The discussion eventually turned to the impending film and its "disappointingly odd little man" of a director. Calista sipped from her glass and shook her head.

"I almost pity Mr. Weber. He's already made an enemy of Tilda, something I wouldn't recommend to anyone."

Decklan raised his glass. "Indeed. The man can write a screenplay, I'll grant him that, but as a human being, he's an undeniable failure. When I first met Vincent in person before the flight from Los Angeles, I asked where everyone else was. I assumed he would have a team, an entourage, coming along with him. He looked at me as if I had grown two heads, rolled his eyes, and claimed working alone was part of his *process.* Now I know better. It's that most people can't stand him. I assume the studio tolerates Vincent because his films make them some money, but those films were small projects compared to this. To be honest, I'm thinking of pulling the plug on the whole thing. Calista feels the same. We're both increasingly uncertain over allowing him access to our story. Contractually, I still have right of refusal."

"And I'll support Decklan one hundred percent should he choose to use it!" Calista declared. "A man with Vincent Weber's attitude, his sense of misplaced superiority – you just can't trust someone like that."

Another bottle was opened. The three moved into the main living area that was dominated by a massive stone rock fireplace and the ceiling-to-floor windows that overlooked Deer Harbor and the islands beyond. The light of the moon danced atop the water's smooth surface. Calista rested her head against Decklan's chest and let out a long sigh.

"Oh, how I missed this view."

As more wine flowed, Adele detailed the important events of her life that had took place during Decklan and Calista's absence from the islands. She spoke of the horrific mystery of the body discovered stuffed into the crab pot near Ripple Island, the epidemic of drug overdoses detailed in her newspaper, the destruction of Roland Soros's yacht, the death of Lucas Pine's father, the girl in Olga who the San Juan locals continued to help so she could receive the treatment her debilitating medical condition required, and of Adele's unexpected and increasingly close friendship with Tilda Ashland.

After listening intently to every word with wide eyes and a proud smile, Calista poured the last of the wine from the second bottle into the glasses and then lifted her own glass high. "I propose a toast. To our brilliant and talented Adele, who is living her life as it was meant to be lived: without fear, without regret, helping others, and with a taste for adventure. We are blessed to call her a friend."

The three glasses clinked together. The noise echoed throughout the house. Adele finished her wine, thanked Calista for the meal, hugged both her and Decklan, and then made her way upstairs to the guest room. After brushing her teeth and washing her face, she lay down on the bed and looked out at the sliver of moon visible through the bedroom window.

Adele's body was tired, but she couldn't sleep. Her mind raced with worry over Dan Walser, his relationship with Yuri Popov, and what those two men were planning to do to Lucas and Roland. Her eyes widened in the dark when she considered the possibility it wasn't just Lucas and Roland they were coming for. Why not her? After all, she had convinced Roland to donate the Cattle Point property to the county, cutting off Yuri's direct line of influence into the area's future business development and its considerable profits.

The sudden loss of that kind of income potential would infuriate a man like Yuri Popov.

Adele was certain that situation was directly linked to Sergei Kozlov's bizarre confrontation with Lucas the morning he was shot. Though the link remained unknown, she intended to find out what it was. That discovery would begin with her conversation with Lucas tomorrow.

Until then, she would try to get some much-needed sleep.

Chapter 5

"How's the coffee?"

Adele looked up and nodded. "It's good, thank you."

"And the ride over from Deer Harbor?"

Again, Adele nodded. "Yeah, it was smooth waters all the way back and ear-to-ear grins from Decklan behind the wheel of his boat. It's great having Calista and him back on the islands."

Lucas sat down. He had already mentioned how he was running on no sleep. He was anxious to hear what Adele had to say about Dan Walser, though. The kitchen was in disarray. Adele noted the half-empty bottle of whiskey next to the sink. Lucas had just showered, but she could still smell a hint of alcohol seeping from his pores. It was just after nine in the morning, and he hadn't even dressed yet. He was still in his robe and slippers.

"Sorry about the mess. I've been busy." Lucas grimaced. "Actually, that's not true. I've been more worried about the investigation than I let on. The timing couldn't be worse given the upcoming election. You've seen how the media treats law enforcement. Every time one of us has to use deadly force, they're presumed guilty until proven innocent. I have a slew of unanswered requests for interviews from reporters including one from Bellingham, another in Seattle, and even someone from New York. They all want me to give them a statement which I know is really their way of giving me the rope to hang myself with. Why the hell did Sergei have to point that gun at me? What was he thinking?"

Adele shook her head. "I don't know, but I do intend to try and found out. I think Dan Walser is somehow involved. I met him the other day in Roche Harbor. He was with Yuri Popov."

Lucas nearly dropped his cup of coffee onto the table. "What? Yuri is here on the islands?"

Adele nodded. "Yeah, or at least he was. I spoke with him."

Lucas's eyes blinked rapidly as he leaned forward over the table. "And they were together – Popov and Walser? You're sure of it?"

"No doubt about it. Walser showed up first. Yuri was right behind him."

"What did they want?"

"Walser said he had questions about the shooting and wondered why I hadn't written anything about it yet. Popov wanted to know where Roland was."

Lucas scratched at the stubble on his chin. "Did you tell them?"

"Tell them what?"

"Where Roland is."

Adele found it odd Lucas was focusing on the topic of Roland and not first wanting to know what Walser asked her regarding the shooting. "Why would I do that?"

Lucas shrugged. "Where is he?"

"Who? Roland? I don't know. He wouldn't tell me."

As soon as she said it, Adele knew it was a mistake. She had just admitted to knowing Roland had taken off. Lucas stared at her. She glanced down at her coffee.

"Are you covering for him?"

Adele looked up. Lucas waited for an answer.

"I don't know what you're talking about. Roland left. That's all I know."

"Left where?"

Adele sighed. "I told you – I don't know. He was leaving the islands for a while. That's all he said."

"How?"

"How what?"

"How did he leave? Was it by boat? A plane? Did he drive his car onto the ferry?"

Adele glared at Lucas. "What's with the interrogation? Why aren't you asking me about Walser?"

Lucas continued to stare at Adele. "I intend to. You were the one who mentioned Roland."

Adele shook her head. "No, I told you that Yuri Popov mentioned Roland. I wasn't the one who brought him up. I was just answering your question."

"Then why aren't you answering my question about how Roland left? Did he drive away, fly away, or float?"

"Lucas, why is it so important that you know? Isn't it Roland's own business how and where he chooses to go?"

" I guess, but why is it so important that you keep it from me?"

"This isn't about Roland. This is about the shooting. It's about Dan Walser and Yuri Popov and what part they might have played in it."

Lucas smacked the table with the bottom half of his clenched fist. "And who was it Yuri wanted to locate? It was Roland, right? Maybe there's a connection you'd rather not consider."

"Or maybe you're just looking to blame Roland – *again.*"

The history between Adele, Roland, and Lucas was a complicated one but Adele had thought that after Roland had donated his Cattle Point property to the county last winter so a drug treatment facility could be built in honor of Lucas's father, the late Dr. Edmund Pine, a more lasting truce between the two men would follow. It seemed that truce, if it had ever really existed, was now over. Lucas was as suspicious of Roland as ever.

"My asking about Roland has nothing to do with you and him, Adele. I promise."

"Then what is it?"

Lucas stood up, went over to the counter, and put his cup in the sink. When he answered, he still had his back to Adele.

"I can't tell you that."

Adele attempted to process the multitude of possibilities that answer could mean. Who would have the authority to order a county sheriff on what they could and could not say?

"Is it related to Walser and the shooting investigation?"

Lucas remained in front of the sink, his hands gripping the counter. "No. This just involves Roland."

Adele had been concerned about how Lucas was holding up. Now she was even more concerned about what kind of trouble Roland could be in. Lucas turned around.

"If you have any idea where he went, you really should tell me. You already know he has Yuri after him, but Yuri isn't the only one. I'd be out there looking for Roland myself, asking around, but I'm on administrative leave until the inquiry is concluded. I'm not really the sheriff right now."

"The same inquiry that has you sidelined is the same inquiry being headed by Dan Walser. And if Walser is working for Yuri like I think he is then basically it's Yuri's inquiry. You do realize that, right?"

Lucas stuck his hands into the pockets of his robe. "Sure, I know. Just because I'm not on the job doesn't mean I've lost all ability to put two-and-two together."

"So, what are you going to do about it?"

"For now? Nothing. I'll wait, watch, and listen. Chancee and Gunther will keep an eye on Walser and his investigation. If I were to go off half-cocked, making accusations about Walser working for Yuri, I'd be playing right into their hands. They know you and I talk. When they approached you at Roche Harbor, they were counting on you telling me about it. They think I'll confront Walser first thing. They want me to. Instead, I'll sit tight and wait. Let them make a mistake. When they do, I'll be ready."

Adele was impressed. Bathrobe and slippers aside, Lucas hadn't completely lost his head.

"What if they *don't* make a mistake? What if they're able to successfully weaponize the investigation against you?"

"Given Sergei's criminal record, and the fact he was armed the morning of the shooting, it doesn't seem likely. They'll be those who wonder why he was shot in the head and not the chest and if I followed protocol after the shooting. All that stuff gets looked at, but none of it should influence the council enough that they actually find me at fault for anything. That's not saying when you told me Walser and Yuri were connected I didn't get a pucker in my backside. Believe me, I did. I'm worried. Something's up and, as usual, Yuri Popov is most likely pulling the strings."

"If you weren't on administrative leave, where would be the first place you'd look to try and find out what Yuri is up to?"

Lucas sat back down at the table and wagged a finger at Adele. "No, don't even think about it."

Adele played dumb. "What do you mean?"

Lucas's eyes narrowed. "You know *exactly* what I mean. Don't go running around in detective mode again. I already told you the plan. Sit tight and see what their next play is."

"That's *your* plan. I never said it was going to be mine." Adele flashed a smile. "Besides, when did I ever do what you told me?"

Lucas grunted. "You have a point there. Still, to have Yuri Popov make the trip from Vancouver to the islands personally seems odd. And you said it was just him and Walser – no entourage of goons?"

Adele nodded. "That's right – just those two."

Lucas tapped the table with the tip of a finger. "See, that's a different pattern of behavior for him, which concerns me. Yuri Popov is an old man, a creature of habit. He doesn't emerge from whatever cave in Vancouver he conducts his business from often. Yet here he is personally trying to track down Roland, and he brings along a former state cop with him who happens to be leading the inquiry into the Sergei Kozlov shooting – a shooting that took place mere months out from an election that will leave me with or without a job."

Adele was a strong believer in cause and effect. She suspected these things were all connected, including the ones involving Roland.

"And don't forget the thing you say you can't tell me about Roland. That took place at the same time as Yuri and Walser's arrival as well."

Lucas frowned. "Huh. You're right. I hadn't considered that could be related. But that would mean…"

His voice trailed off. Adele leaned forward.

"What would it mean, Lucas? Tell me. Look, we're all involved in this. I have a right to know."

Lucas put his elbows on the table and propped his chin on his folded hands. "Did Roland ever mention anything to you about money problems – issues with the bank, that sort of thing?"

The question caught Adele off guard. She tried to hide her surprise with a shrug.

"The Cattle Point project spread him thin for a while, but he never indicated anything to suggest it was serious."

"Roland donated that property to the county, though, right? So how did he hope to make back all the money he sunk into it?"

"I don't know. It wasn't my place to pry that far into Roland's financial dealings, and he doesn't like to talk about money."

"And why do you think that is?"

Adele felt Lucas was interrogating her again. She scowled and shook her head.

"That's Roland's business, not mine…or yours."

"Adele, Roland owns the only bank in the San Juan Islands. That comes with a whole slew of regulations – *federal* regulations. I'm not the one going after him. Fact is, I'd like to help, but my own hands are tied with the shooting inquiry."

"Who's going after Roland? C'mon, tell me what you know."

Lucas glanced up at the ceiling. He took a deep breath then looked at Adele.

"There was a man here at the house this morning. He came unannounced, asked me some questions, and then left not more than twenty minutes before you arrived. He said his name was Randall Eaton. He's an FDIC compliance investigator who works from the field office in Seattle."

"Why was he here?" Adele asked.

"Two reasons. The first was a matter of professional courtesy. I'm the county sheriff, so he was notifying me of his investigation. The second was he wanted my help in locating Roland. I told him I didn't know where Roland was. By the look he gave, I'm pretty sure he didn't believe me."

"So, Roland has the Feds investigating his banking business, and you have the state reviewing the Sergei shooting. And both of these are happening at the exact same time? That's quite a coincidence, don't you think?"

"Maybe, maybe not. I'll tell you this, though. Eaton mentioned Yuri. Not directly, but he asked me if I knew of any potential relationship between Roland and organized crime."

"What did you say?"

Lucas shrugged. "It was a question Eaton already had the answer to. He was seeing if I could be trusted, so I told him the truth – at least some of it. I said there had been rumors but nothing concrete to suggest Roland had an *ongoing* relationship with anyone in organized crime. I stuck to present tense so Eaton couldn't circle back around and accuse me of misleading him. I just hope Roland isn't still involved with Yuri because if he is, that will give Eaton a whole lot of ammo to go after him – hard."

"How bad could it be?"

Lucas sighed. "Real bad. The Feds could close down the bank. There could be fines, even prison. Roland would lose everything, and I mean *everything*."

Adele rubbed her temples. "My god, to lose his family's legacy, everything his grandfather built. It would destroy him."

"I know. It would destroy anyone. Roland's in a heap of trouble, Adele. That has to be the reason for his sudden departure. Now it's just a matter of who finds him first. Will it be Yuri or the Feds? A bullet to the head or years behind bars?"

Adele's eyes flashed fire. "That's *not* going to happen. We won't let it."

Lucas was silent. Adele took that as a sign of his uncertainty over what the immediate future might hold for any of them. She refused to just sit back and wait for the answer.

"I need to go. I have an edition of the newspaper to finish. It'll mention the shooting but not much. We'll let the other media swim in speculation."

"There'll probably be some who think you're doing that to protect me."

Adele waved her hand. "I don't care. This is our home. We don't eat our own."

Before leaving, Adele turned around and looked Lucas up and down. "You need to get dressed. Stop spending so much time inside this house. People will start to wonder if you're cracking under the pressure. Get out there and remind them you're still their sheriff. Look the part."

Adele opened the door, stepped outside, and closed it behind her. She glanced up. Dark clouds were rolling in; rain was coming. She moved from the backyard to the front and froze.

A dark-haired female reporter dressed smartly in a blouse and skirt was holding a microphone while leaning against a white news van that had a satellite bolted to its roof. An older, overweight cameraman with a bad comb-over stood directly behind her. As soon as they noticed Adele, they both jogged across the street. When Adele started to walk toward her car, the reporter called out after her.

"Ma'am if I could please have a word with you. Do you have a comment regarding rumors the sheriff had a history of intimidation against the deceased, Mr. Kozlov, and that the shooting might have been personally motivated?"

Adele intended to ignore the reporter, get into her car, and drive away.

"Ma'am, is it true a full criminal investigation is now being considered against the sheriff due to allegations of abuse of power? That the sheriff had already intended to kill Sergei Kozlov prior to that morning's shooting?"

Adele whirled around. She felt her heart thumping inside her chest.

"*What?*"

The reporter stuck the microphone under Adele's nose. Adele brushed it aside.

"Get that thing out of my face. I have no idea what you're talking about. Who did you hear this crap from?"

"From a source close to the investigation, Ms. Plank. How do you respond?"

Again, the microphone was put under Adele's nose, and again, she pushed it away. "Who are you and how do you know my name?"

"Marianne Rocha, Action Five News Seattle. You're local reporter Adele Plank, correct?"

Adele nodded. "Yeah, that's right, and I have nothing to say to you."

"So that's a no-comment regarding the sheriff and allegations of abuse of power and premeditated murder?"

The microphone bumped up against Adele's cheek. She ripped it out of the reporter's hand and flung it to the ground. "I told you to get that thing out of my face!"

Marianne stepped in front of Adele in an attempt to block her from reaching the MINI.

"Has your newspaper been aiding the sheriff in a cover-up of his illegal activities? Has he threatened you or are you being paid off by him?"

Adele heard Lucas's front door creak open. She turned her head and saw him standing on the front porch still wearing his robe and slippers.

"Adele, you OK? Are these two bothering you?"

The cameraman panned the camera toward Lucas as Marianne reached down, picked up the microphone, and then scampered across the front yard. "Sheriff Pine, I'm Marianne Rocha, Action Five News Seattle. If I could have just a moment of your time, I'd like to get your response regarding allegations of wrongdoing now being leveled against you."

Lucas glanced at Adele. She pointed at his house while mouthing the words, 'go back inside.' Lucas backed away from the Seattle reporter.

"I have no idea what you're talking about. You can't be on my property. Please leave. Thank you."

"Are you going to resign your position, Sheriff? Will you be ending your campaign?"

Marianne Rocha was clearly baiting Lucas hoping to get an outburst from him that would be caught on camera. Adele continued to motion for him to get inside. Lucas hesitated, leveling a look at the reporter that made Adele fear things were about to take an ugly turn. She breathed a sigh of relief when he retreated without saying anything more and closed the door.

With the reporter and her cameraman still standing at the bottom of Lucas's front porch, Adele got into her car and sped off. A few minutes later, her phone rang. She glanced down and saw the call was from Bess Jenkins, the seventy-five-year-old co-owner of the *Island Gazette.* Adele pulled over to take the call.

"Adele, thank goodness you picked up! We're being raided!"

"What are you talking about Bess? Who is being raided?"

Bess's voice was cracking from the strain of whatever had her so upset. "The newspaper – he's here in our office right now! He showed up with a warrant, and he's turning the place upside down. Taking our physical files, the hard drives from the computers, we don't have anything for this week's edition. He took it all!"

Avery, Bess's husband, was yelling in the background. "What gives him the right? I think Avery is going to have a heart attack over this. I mean it! He's furious. You know how sick he's been. This is going to kill him."

"Bess, who showed up with a warrant?"

Adele had to wait for a response as Bess pleaded for Avery to sit down before he dropped dead. Adele repeated her question.

"It's that interim sheriff. The one called Walser. He's boxing everything up right now."

Bess's voice lowered. "He's asking about you, Adele."

Adele's jaw clenched. "That's fine, Bess. I'm on my way. You tell Walser I'm coming."

Chapter 6

"Ah, there you are, Ms. Plank. I'm sorry we have to see each other under these circumstances. I'm done here, but I'd like you to come by the Sheriff's Office in about an hour for an interview. I strongly suggest you show up voluntarily."

Walser's arrogant tone made Adele grind her teeth. He stood outside the door of the *Gazette*, a box stuffed with files and computer discs under his arm. Adele's first instinct was to punch him in the middle of his fat, smirking face. She clenched her fists, relishing how good that would feel.

"Ms. Plank, you look like you want to hit somebody."

Adele's jaw clenched as she pointed at Walser. "You like scaring old people? Tearing up their place of business? What gives you the right?"

"There's no need for this to turn confrontational. I'm just a man doing his job. I'll see you in an hour."

The *Gazette's* front door was flung open, revealing a red-faced and trembling Avery Jenkins. The longtime owner of the newspaper needed the use of a walker to move around these days. Avery gripped the walker with one hand while jabbing a finger at Walser with the other.

"Adele won't be taking a step inside your damn office without a lawyer at her side, I can promise you that! Now get the hell out of here. This is private property!"

Bess tried to pull Avery back inside but he shrugged off the attempt. Walser adjusted the box under his arm and shook his head.

"Mr. Jenkins, I showed you the warrant. My search of the premises was perfectly legal. Now, I know you folks out on these islands like to think you can live by your own rules free from the laws of the mainland, but that just isn't so. You have to answer to those same laws just like everyone else. Need I remind you I'm conducting an investigation into a man's death?"

The corners of Avery's mouth twitched, and his eyes widened. "What does my newspaper have to do with your investigation? I'll tell you – nothing. You wish to speak of laws? Fine! Need I remind *you* of the freedom of the press?"

Walser glanced at Adele. "My visit here wasn't necessarily about you specifically or your business, Mr. Jenkins."

Bess forced herself past her husband so she could join him in snarling at Walser. "It isn't enough that you show up unannounced and turn our office upside down, huh? No, now you have to threaten Adele as well. You're a disgrace to the badge, Mr. Walser. I don't know what foul current washed you up onto our shores, but you listen, and you listen good. You made some enemies today, and we won't stop until you're forced back to whatever hole it was you crawled out from."

Walser puffed out his chest. "You shouldn't talk to me like that, Mrs. Jenkins. I might decide to stick around. I'm starting to like it here. I think this place has real potential."

Avery shuffled forward until he stood nose to nose with Walser. "I told you to leave. That warrant doesn't give you the right to loiter or trespass. Now go."

Fearing Walser might actually do something to hurt the much older Avery, Adele moved between the two men. "I'll be at your office in an hour Mr. Walser. I have some questions for you as well."

Walser frowned. "I won't comment on an ongoing investigation, Ms. Plank. You'll answer *my* questions. That's it."

Adele nodded. "Sure, that's fine. I'll just put that down as a 'no comment' in the article."

Walser's eyes narrowed. "What article?"

Adele enjoyed hearing the uncertainty in Walser's voice. He likely thought the raid on the newspaper would temporarily prevent any new issues of the paper from coming out. He was wrong.

"The article in the next issue of *The Island Gazette* of course - it'll be out soon."

Walser eyed Adele, Avery, and Bess and then abruptly turned and left. Bess let out a long sigh and gave Adele's shoulder a gentle squeeze.

"Thank you, Adele. You handled that well."

Avery grunted. "That is a man hiding some serious wrongdoing. I'm sure of it." He looked at Adele. "How do you plan on coming out with another issue of the paper? Walser just left with our layout and print software and all our hard drives. We're dead in the water here."

Adele shrugged. "We'll figure something out. Whatever Walser is up to, he's not going to get away with it."

Bess motioned for Adele and Avery to follow her inside. Adele saw the extent of the damage left behind by Walser's visit. Papers covered the floor. Drawers had been yanked out. Computers had been pried open and lay on their side. It hadn't been so much a search and seizure as it was a complete tossing of the place.

Avery leaned against his walker and shook his head. "The bastard barged in here and treated us like criminals. Why would he do that? We've been in business all these years, and I've never experienced anything like this before."

Bess wrapped her arm around her husband. "Clearly he was trying to intimidate us. We won't let him. I'll start to clean up."

Adele held up her hand. "Wait. Leave it like it is. We need to take some photos first."

Avery grinned. "Ah, that's right. Show everyone exactly what Walser did. Let the community know of the problem that now walks among us."

Bess looked at Adele. "But we can't go to print. He took everything. We can replace it all, but that will take weeks."

Adele used her phone to take the first picture of the mess Walser had left. She continued moving around the office taking more photos while replying to Bess's concerns.

"Walser took what we need for the *paper* version. We can still do the issue online with instructions that people print it off and share with others who don't have Internet access. Everything you had here on your hard drives for the online edition Jose has on his computer at his home. He handles all the online stuff for us already. We just need to give him the content. I'd say Walser's visit here today gave us all the content we'll need for the next issue."

Jose had been in charge of *The Island Gazette's* online presence for some time even as he continued to oversee the paper's physical distribution all across the San Juan Islands. Since Adele first met him a few years ago, he remained a man who said little but did much. She was confident in his ability to quickly put together an online-only version for them.

After taking several pictures, Adele helped Bess clean up while Avery sat down in a chair to rest. Within minutes he was nodding off despite the activity going on around him. Bess gave him a loving look as she shook her head.

"Poor thing, it's going to take him a while to recover from all the stress of today."

Adele knew Bess was right. Every week Avery appeared to be getting a little weaker. And yet, he hadn't backed down from Walser. Adele hoped there was still some fight left in her friend and business partner and that it would be enough to keep him going for a while longer.

After the office was cleaned up and Jose had been informed by phone of the plans for an online-only edition of the paper Adele prepared to leave for her meeting with Walser. Avery woke up and pushed himself to his feet.

"Let me go with you."

Adele shook her head. "No, you stay with Bess. She needs you here."

It was a small, well-intentioned lie and Avery made clear he knew it right away. He gave Adele a half-grin.

"Uh-huh. I think what you're really telling me is to stay out of your way and let Bess take care of me." When Adele started to protest, Avery shrugged.

"No need to say anything more. You're right. I would just slow you down. Still, I think having an attorney with you isn't a bad idea. I can make some calls."

"I'll be fine, Avery. In fact, my plan is to be the one asking Walser most the questions."

"There's a council meeting tomorrow. It's likely they're the ones who assigned Walser to investigate the shooting. I say we show up there and start asking *them* some questions as well."

Adele told Avery that sounded like a good idea. She gave him a hug and told him to get some rest. Bess walked her outside and closed the door behind them.

"I know you sense how dangerous this Walser is, Adele. Avery is right to want to have someone come with you. Clearly, Walser isn't here to investigate the shooting. There's some other reason that appears to involve you. What that reason might be, I have no idea beyond knowing it's trouble. Sheriff Pine can't intervene due to the investigation, meaning you're even more exposed to whatever threat Walser poses. You should cancel the meeting with him. That would give us more time to prepare."

"I know he's trying to lay some trap. Just like I know he's counting on me to cancel. I think that's what he wants. It'll make me look like I'm hiding something. Well, I'm not, and Walser needs to know that, just like he needs to know I'm not afraid of him."

Adele was halfway to her car when Bess called out. "Will you be coming back here after the meeting?"

"No, I have to go see someone else and then put the Walser article together for Jose. I'll check in with you tomorrow." Adele waved goodbye and left. She was opening the door to her car when a flash of red caught her eye. It was a sign staked next to a tree along the sidewalk about a half-block down from where she was parked. She walked toward it, squinting as she tried to confirm what it said.

VOTE DAN WALSER FOR COUNTY SHERIFF

Adele read the sign over and over, hoping it might actually say something else. She had read it right. Adele took a picture.

Dan Walser wasn't just investigating Lucas. He was planning to replace him.

Chapter 7

"I just saw a sign that says you're running for sheriff. Given you're investigating the current sheriff, I'd call that a serious conflict of interest."

Walser appeared surprised. "I have no idea what you're talking about. I didn't put up any sign."

Adele sat down inside of Lucas's office – the one Walser was now using as his own. "I'm sure there are other rooms here at the station you could have used. Why take this one?"

Walser smiled as he leaned back in Lucas's chair. "Logistically, it just seemed like the most appropriate choice. I understand your need to try and defend your friend. I'm not here to take Sheriff Pine's job. I'm simply doing mine."

"Then where did the election sign come from?"

"I don't know. I assure you I'll take a look for myself once our business here is concluded."

Adele sat up straight in her chair. "I want to make it clear I know I don't have to talk to you. You requesting I stop by isn't a court summons. It has no authority to force me to be here. I can leave at any time."

Walser shrugged. "I never said otherwise."

Adele hated seeing someone else behind Lucas's desk. It looked wrong, like dark oil corrupting clear and clean water.

"Ask your questions. I have things to do and stories to write."

Walser cleared his throat. "You're really going to attempt another issue of your little paper? I thought you were just trying to threaten me. How do you intend to do that given I just confiscated all of your software and hard drives?"

Adele locked eyes with Walser. "Don't worry, I'll manage. Now ask your questions."

Walser folded his hands together while Adele's eyes continued to bore into his. He looked away first, cleared his throat again, and nodded.

"Fine, let's do that. What can you tell me about Sheriff Pine's relationship to Sergei Kozlov?"

Adele paused, wondering where Walser was attempting to lead her. "Nothing."

Walser frowned. "Nothing? I reviewed the incident reports, Ms. Plank. At one time, didn't you accuse Mr. Kozlov of shooting at your car? And wasn't it Sheriff Pine who was the first to respond to that accusation in a law enforcement capacity?"

Adele remembered the incident well. It took place two years ago at a restaurant parking lot following a dinner with Roland Soros. It was the first time she had seen Sergei Kozlov. He had been speaking with Roland while the both of them stood in the darkness behind her car.

"If you read the incident reports, then you know as much as I do."

Walser smirked. "Come now, Ms. Plank, let's not pretend that's even remotely true. You do make an important point, though. It is incident *reports* – plural. There isn't just *one* involving Sheriff Pine and Sergei Kozlov. Those two have a well-established history. From that first accusation of someone shooting at your car to further accusations of drug trafficking, it seems the sheriff initiated an increasingly aggressive campaign against Mr. Kozlov."

"Sergei was a criminal. Lucas is the sheriff. They have a history because Lucas is doing his job trying to keep the people on these islands safe from people like Sergei Kozlov."

"Hmmm, that might be true, but as I reviewed the reports, there seems to be a common link tying Mr. Kozlov and Sheriff Pine together."

"And what link is that?"

Walser pointed at Adele. "You."

Adele scoffed. "Me? Are you attempting to link me to Sergei's criminal behavior?"

Walser leaned forward. "Sheriff Pine's own records don't conclusively link Sergei Kozlov to criminal activity. It's *suggested* but far from proven. What is easier to make out is this pattern of harassment by the sheriff against Mr. Kozlov that often included you in one way or another. With that in mind, please explain your relationship with the sheriff."

Adele shook her head. "I don't have to explain anything. My relationship with Lucas, Sheriff Pine, has absolutely nothing to do with what happened to Sergei Kozlov."

"You and the sheriff have grown close since your arrival to these islands a few years earlier, correct?"

Adele thought of leaving but didn't want to give Walser the satisfaction of knowing he had rattled her. She kept talking.

"Sure. We're friends."

Walser's chin dipped toward his chest. "Just friends? The sheriff is a good-looking man. Tall, athletic, I understand he was quite a football player."

Adele folded her arms but said nothing. Walser waited. He appeared to be enjoying Adele's sudden silence.

"Ms. Plank, are you attracted to Sheriff Pine? Do the two of you have a sexual relationship?"

This time Adele avoided Walser's gaze. She knew that was a mistake. He would take that as a sign of guilt, but she couldn't help it.

"We're friends."

Walser smiled and nodded. "I see. And what about Roland Soros? Are you just friends with him as well?"

Adele bit down on her lower lip. She hadn't expected Walser to ask her about Roland. For the first time since sitting down, she felt the stirrings of panic.

"What does Roland have to do with any of this?"

"You tell me, Ms. Plank."

Adele decided a bit of verbal offense would make for a better defense. "And what is *your* relation to Yuri Popov? Are you working for him?"

Walser leaned back in his chair. "I have no idea what you're talking about. Just answer my question regarding your relationship with Roland Soros."

"I know that Roland had dealings with Yuri Popov – the same man I recently saw you with on the docks at Roche Harbor."

"Again, I have no idea what you're talking about. I did see you in Roche Harbor. Of course, I recall that, but I was there alone. Now, this relationship you say Roland had with Yuri Popov. I need you to elaborate on that."

Adele could hear the frustration in Walser's voice. She hadn't broken down under his scrutiny, and now she was pushing back. He hadn't expected her to be so resilient.

"I don't think so. I'm certain you already know of that relationship, and I intend to explain how in the next issue of *The Island Gazette*."

Walser sighed loudly. "Go ahead, Ms. Plank, spread your wild accusations. It won't help. You refuse to explain your relationship with Roland Soros and Sheriff Pine. That will be duly noted in my investigation. And are you aware Mr. Soros has gone missing? Nobody seems to know where he is. It's a troubling situation given a man of his importance to this community. Perhaps you've witnessed recent tension between Mr. Soros and Sheriff Pine?"

Adele shook her head. "You've got to be kidding. Is that the direction you're going? Accusing the sheriff of having something to do with Roland's absence? You're pathetic. This inquiry, investigation, whatever you want to call it – it's a joke."

Walser's jaw tightened. He leaned further forward. "I didn't say Mr. Soros was *absent.* I said he disappeared. At the very least, that suggests the possibility of foul play."

Adele stood up. "We're done here, Mr. Walser. This will be the last time I speak to you alone."

Walser stood as well. The smirk returned.

"That is probably a good idea, Ms. Plank. In fact, you might want to start looking for a good attorney. This whole situation appears to be heading toward a review by a grand jury. If it reaches that point, they will no doubt want to talk to you as well."

A tight knot formed in Adele's stomach. She knew she had done nothing wrong, but with Walser having so much influence over the investigation into the shooting, she feared wrong and right meant far less than the perception Walser was working so hard to create. That perception could mean everything as Walser continued to craft a false narrative meant to destroy Lucas, Roland, and her as well.

The first realization brought about a second one. "You *are* working for Yuri. He's trying to punish us – the ones he blames for taking the Cattle Point project away from him."

Walser's gaze briefly fell to his desk. In her mind, Adele let out a triumphant shout. She was on the right track. The shooting investigation was just a cover for Yuri's attempted revenge. Adele's voice rose as her confidence returned.

"When I find out how Yuri forced Sergei to sacrifice himself, I'll prove the link between you and Yuri as well. The shooting that brought you here was a setup. I'm certain of it. You're in a hole of your own lies, and I'm going to bury you in it."

Walser clapped. "Bravo. That's quite a story you've created. Good luck with it. Enjoy your freedom while it lasts, Ms. Plank because it likely won't last long."

Adele rapped the top of the desk with her knuckles. "Right back at you. If your plan was to have me come in here and be intimidated - you failed. If you think it'll stop me from finding out the truth about why you're *really* here, you're wrong. Go ahead with your pretend investigation. I'll be doing a real one. And you know what? You can read about it soon, just like everyone else – including the authorities."

Walser continued to grin, but his eyes were ice. "You have a mouth on you for such a young thing. I'll give you that. You're forgetting something very important, though. As of right now, I am the authority here on the islands. Not Sheriff Pine. Not Roland Soros. *Me.* I'll be in touch, Ms. Plank."

Adele left the office and walked quickly down the hall into the reception area. Samantha Boyler looked up from behind her desk, smiled, and then stood up.

"Oh! I almost forgot to give you back that tablecloth I borrowed. I washed it up good. The wine stain came out fine."

Samantha held a folded white cloth over the reception desk. Adele had never seen it before because she had never borrowed anything from Samantha. She glanced up at the camera that hung from the ceiling directly behind the reception desk as she reached for the cloth.

"Thank you, Samantha. I had forgotten all about it. You take care."

Samantha's smile was forced. She stared at the tablecloth in Adele's hand before looking up. Adele saw fear in her eyes.

"You too, Adele. Say hello to Avery and Bess for me."

Adele said she would and then walked outside. A warm breeze blew across her face. The street was choked with summer traffic and smelled of exhaust and saltwater. She had to wait for a gap in the line of vehicles driving by to walk across the street to her MINI. Once she was behind the wheel, she unfolded the cloth and found a piece of paper hidden inside with a message written on it.

Need to talk with you in private. No phones. Tonight @ bookstore. 8:00 p.m. Suze will be expecting us.

Suze was the nickname for Suzanne Blatt, the owner of Island Books and one of Adele's most trusted friends. A meeting at the bookstore would provide a safe place where she could find out what Samantha was so desperate to share. Until then, she would remain in her car across from the Sheriff's Office waiting and watching.

Adele had promised Walser she would bury him with the truth.

She intended to keep that promise.

Chapter 8

Suze greeted Adele with a wide smile and a big hug just inside the entrance to her bookstore. Despite creeping up on sixty, she looked the same as the day when Adele had first met her three years earlier. The short, curly hair remained free of gray, the blue eyes were just as bright and friendly, and the same orthopedic tennis shoes still adorned her feet.

"Come on in. I just made us a fresh pot of coffee. Samantha's not here yet."

Suze closed the door, and then peered through the window at the street outside. "I hope she's OK. She sounded nervous when she called. She said she needed a safe place to talk with you. Do you know what this is about?"

Adele shook her head. "No. Do you?"

Suze stepped back from the window. "No. If I had to guess I would say it's something to do with her work."

Adele was certain Suze's instincts were right. She had personally seen the fear in Samantha's eyes on her way out of the Sheriff's station. A glance down at her phone confirmed it was ten minutes past eight. Samantha was late.

"How is Lucas doing?"

The question hung in the air for a few seconds before Adele realized she hadn't answered. "Oh, he's doing fine. He's pretty occupied with the shooting investigation."

Suze let out a soft grunt. "I imagine he would be. What a terrible thing. I can still hear him yelling for Sergei to drop the weapon and then the sound of that gunshot. When I first heard it, I was certain it was Lucas who had been shot. I hate to admit it, but I was relieved to find out it was someone else who had died. I don't wish death on anyone – but Lucas Pine? He's one of our own."

"There's no shame in that. Everyone who lives here knows Lucas was just doing his job. He would never want to hurt someone unless he felt he absolutely had to."

Adele caught Suze scowling. She asked her what was wrong. Suze glanced outside again.

"I just realized nobody from the Sheriff's Office has interviewed me about the shooting, and as far as I know, none of the other business owners who might have seen or heard what happened have been interviewed either. Doesn't that strike you as odd? What kind of investigation doesn't include input from actual witnesses?"

"An investigation that isn't concerned with the truth of what happened," Adele answered.

Suze's eyes went wide. "Do you really think that's it? Is someone trying to frame the sheriff? Why would anyone want to do such a thing?"

Adele was about to answer when she heard the sound of knocking coming from behind the bookstore. Suze cocked her head.

"Did you hear that?"

Adele nodded.

Suze took a few cautious steps toward the back. Adele followed close behind. Each step made the wood floors creak as they moved between tall shelves stuffed with books. Adele watched Suze reach up and grab a hardcover edition of Tolstoy's *War and Peace* and then hold it in front of her like a weapon. The sound of more knocking made her stiffen. Adele moved past her. "I'll check it out," she said.

Suze pushed the book into Adele's chest. "Here, take this."

Adele was surprised at how heavy the famously lengthy novel felt in her hands. "You want me to defend myself with a copy of *War and Peace*?"

Suze tapped the book's cover. "That's nearly thirteen-hundred pages of classic literature you're carrying there. It's more than enough to knock someone's head off with."

Adele held the book in both hands and shook it. "You're probably right about that."

Another knock caused both women to flinch. Adele turned around and crept into the back room. It was dark. The smell of fresh-brewed coffee hit her nose. Suze bumped up against Adele's shoulder. She apologized and then turned on a light.

The sound of a ringing phone caused Suze to gasp. Adele jumped. Suze took out her phone, answered it, and then smiled. "It's Samantha! She's in the alley asking to be let in."

Suze walked into the bathroom that adjoined the back-room area. Adele heard a door open, and then both Suze and Samantha emerged. Samantha looked at the book in Adele's hands and arched a brow.

"Did I interrupt your book club?"

"Suze thought it would make a good weapon," Adele answered.

Samantha shook her head. "Death by Tolstoy? That's a tough way to go."

The book made a loud thump when Adele dropped it onto the small kitchen table. "Yeah, those multiple epilogues alone can be deadly."

Suze looked at both Adele and Samantha and then started to laugh. "Only in the San Juans can a covert meeting between three women start off with jokes about being killed off by *War and Peace*. God, I love this place! C'mon, let's sit down, have some coffee, and find out the reason for our being here."

Suze poured the coffee and then joined the other two at the table. She looked at Samantha and smiled. "Now, how about you tell us what this is all about."

A small window looked out at the alley. A gap in the curtains revealed how dark it was outside. Samantha reached over, pulled the curtains tight and then glanced at Adele.

"I waited to come until after I knew you would already be here. I didn't want anyone to think we arrived together. I'm pretty sure Walser is suspicious of me. The whole vibe in the office is getting really weird. Every time he shows up there I feel like this black cloud comes with him. He has no business using the sheriff's office, kicking his feet up on the desk like he owns the place."

Adele took a sip of coffee. It was rich and strong, the way she liked it. Suze always made good coffee.

"I feel the same way about Walser. Something is really off with him, and the fact he's the one in charge of looking into the Sergei Kozlov shooting could end up being a very serious problem not just for Lucas but for all of us."

Suze looked over the brim of her cup. "What do you mean?"

Adele tipped her head toward Samantha. "I want to hear what she has to say before I share what I think."

Samantha removed her glasses to clean them. After slipping them back on she took a deep breath, glanced at both Adele and Suze, and then nodded.

"Here's the deal. Yesterday someone came into the office. She was very tall, attractive, and rather intimidating in her blouse, skirt, and four-inch heels. I'd guess late thirties or early forties. She looked at me as if I was an annoying child and then demanded to see Walser. I asked what her name was and if she had an appointment. She didn't tell me. She just repeated her demand to see Walser. Before I could say anything else, Walser poked his head around the corner and then his eyes got real big like a pair of dinner plates. It was obvious he knew who she was. He walked out acting real nervous and then motioned for her to follow him back to his office. Ten minutes later, the woman goes by my desk without looking at me or saying anything and leaves. She never signed in, never told me her name, and Walser hasn't mentioned her since. What he *did* do, though, was come back out to the reception area looking like he had seen a ghost. His face was pale. He was sweating and was clutching a piece of paper in his hand. Whatever was said between him and that woman shook him up. He said he had to go meet with a member of the council and took off. I didn't see him for the rest of the day, which was fine by me, but I was sure curious as to who that woman was."

"What did you do?" Suze asked.

Samantha swirled the coffee in her cup. "That piece of paper I told you about? The one I saw Walser holding in his hand? Well, that gave me an idea. I went into his office and found his notepad. I did just like you see in those spy movies. I rubbed across the page with a pencil to see what he had written on it."

Adele's eyes widened. "Really? Did it work?"

Samantha withdrew a piece of paper and slid it across the table. "You tell me."

Adele picked up the paper. Suze's gaze darted from Samantha to Adele. "What's it say?"

Adele asked if she could keep the paper. Samantha said yes while Suze grew more impatient to find out what the paper said.

"Hey! Keep me in the loop, ladies. C'mon!"

Adele handed her the paper. Suze looked down then looked up and shrugged. "I don't get it. What is Weber?"

"Not what – *who*," Adele replied. "Vincent Weber. He's the director who wants to do the film based on Decklan and Calista. He flew in earlier. He's staying over at Rosario right now."

Suze nodded. "Ah, that's right."

"Yeah, but what does he have to do with Walser?" Samantha asked.

Adele's brows drew together. "Good question. Finding that out will take some time. Until then, we need to prepare for tomorrow night's council meeting. I want a packed house – lots of people there watching and listening."

Suze rested her elbows on the table. "What should we be watching and listening for?"

Adele paused as she considered her next words carefully. "I have reason to suspect Walser is linked to organized crime. Namely, the Russian mafia up in Canada. That's not what really troubles me at this point, though. The thing is, Walser was appointed to his current position by the county council, right? All of the authority he has right now to investigate Lucas and anyone else on these islands was granted to him by the council."

Samantha's sat up straight. "Someone on the council brought Walser here."

Adele nodded. "That's right. There's at least one member who is in on whatever scheme Walser is a part of. During tomorrow night's council meeting I'm going to try and find out who that member is."

Samantha leaned forward. "You said you think Walser might be tied to the Russian mafia. Well, the woman who came into the station, she had a pretty heavy accent, and I'm pretty sure it was Russian. I know the history between the sheriff and Sergei. I'm guessing the woman is involved in that as well. Perhaps she's an associate or even a relative."

Suze stood up. "My goodness, this is definitely a two-cup conversation." She proceeded to refill everyone's coffee and then sat back down while Adele processed the new information Samantha had just provided.

"Samantha, the station has surveillance cameras, right?"

Samantha snapped her fingers. "Right! We have one at the entrance that records everyone who arrives and leaves. I'll pull the tape and get you a copy."

Adele's face tightened. "Be careful. Walser is dangerous. And if we're right, certainly the people he's working for are as well. If he catches you…"

"I know. I'll be careful. I should be able to get you a copy by tomorrow. I'll go in to work early before he comes in and then leave it here for you to pick up."

Adele sensed the bond being forged between the three of them that night and was grateful to have their help. She knew

Suze and Samantha were just as determined to fight back against whatever plans Yuri Popov and Dan Walser were attempting against the islands.

By the time their second cup of coffee was finished the three women had a plan. Samantha would secure a copy of the surveillance footage. She remained adamant about avoiding the use of phones or email.

"If Walser gets approval for a grand jury he'll have full subpoena powers. Anything electronic he'll have access to. If he's looking to take down more than just the sheriff, that's how he'll do it. We'll all be drawn into the conspiracy he's trying to create. Phone contacts, emails, it can all be used to make us appear like accomplices."

"Accomplices to what, though?" Suze asked.

Samantha shrugged. "It doesn't matter. If he gets a grand jury, he can make our lives hell."

Adelle nodded. "She's right. Walser seems to want to pull as many of us into this mess as he can."

Suze put her hand on Adele's arm. "Should we tell the sheriff what we think and about the mysterious Russian woman who showed up at the station?"

Adele shook her head. "He already suspects the same as we do. As for the woman, I need to find out exactly who she is before I present that information to Lucas."

The mention of Lucas made Adele remember something he had recently told her. She turned toward Samantha.

"Has anyone by the name of Randall Eaton come by to speak with Walser?"

Samantha frowned. "No, never heard of him. Why?"

Adele decided to keep what she knew of the FDIC officer to herself, but wondered why Eaton hadn't met with anyone at the Sheriff's Office to inquire about Roland's whereabouts.

"I'm not sure, but if he shows up, please let me know, OK?"

"Yeah, no problem."

The three women stood up. Suze put her hands on her hips.

"Well, what do we do next?"

Adele pointed at Suze. "You get on that phone tree of yours and make sure as many people as possible come to tomorrow night's council meeting. Samantha is going to get a copy of the surveillance footage and drop it off here tomorrow like she said. As for me, I have two things to take care of. The first is to get the next issue of the paper finished. It'll be an online-only version. We're going to try and release it by tomorrow afternoon, so people have time to read it before the council meeting. I'm hoping that'll help them show up to the meeting more informed about what is really going on."

"And what's the second thing you need to take care of?" Samantha asked.

Adele grinned. "Buy a boat."

Chapter 9

"She's beautiful."

Adele meant it. The Chris Craft Lancer's lines were gorgeous. Seventy-two-year-old Gentry Pickett, the lean-faced man who was selling it to her, nodded his approval.

"I appreciate anyone who knows a good thing when they see it, and believe me, this here little boat is a mighty good thing. It took me all of three years to make her right. From bow to stern she's better than the day they pushed her out of the factory. It's twenty-three feet but rides much bigger. That bow cuts through waves like a politician spends money. It's a dry ride, too, if you match the speed to the conditions. She'll do just over thirty-five knots if needed, but loafs along real comfortable at about twenty-five or so which around here is plenty fast to get you anywhere a person needs to go. And it's the hardtop version, which is especially rare - keeps everyone warm and dry when the weather turns nasty."

Adele was happy to stand back and listen to Gentry as he went through the details of his boat. He was like so many other island residents of a similar age – time-worn faces but with bodies and minds that remained both strong and sharp with an undiminished zest for life. Being with him was a welcome reprieve from a hectic morning spent finalizing the online edition of the newspaper.

"Like the ad said, she's a '73. That's the year I returned home from Vietnam. Did two tours as a chopper mechanic over there. Been fixing up old stuff like this ever since I got back. Always had a knack for it. That's the only reason I'm selling. Got my eye on a run-down 1940's era Indian Chief motorcycle a guy is willing to part with over in Bellingham, but he isn't going to give it away. It's begging to be restored right. I need the cash if I'm gonna be able to swing the deal. I'll never get back the work I put into this boat. You never do. Rebuilt the diesel and dropped it in myself. It's rated at two-hundred horsepower with the turbo - tons of torque. The weight of the motor keeps the center of gravity low, and with the big rudder she tracks great and sips fuel while doing it. You'll really notice it around the docks – just point and go. All new electrical, custom windlass, GPS, VHF, wipers, seats, fish box, pole holders, risers, fresh bottom paint, zincs, reinforced stringers, brand new commercial-grade outdrive with duo-prop, and a decent sound system if you're into that sort of thing. She's ready to go. And rest assured there's an inch of hand-laid fiberglass below the waterline - real tough stuff. She'll take a pounding out there and shrug it off like it's nothing. They don't make boats like this anymore. Cost too much. It's all thin-sprayed fiberglass garbage. This boat here? That's old-school American made, just like me."

Adele did the math in her head. Though she was making pretty good money as part owner of the newspaper, the payment on her student loans took a sizeable chunk out of her income each month. Over the last three years, she had managed to save fourteen thousand dollars. Gentry was asking eighteen-thousand for the Chris Craft.

"I'd be offended if you didn't dicker with me a bit," he said.

Adele was grateful for his willingness to negotiate but feared the price difference would remain too great. The problem was that after looking at the boat and learning about all the work that had gone into it, she really, really wanted it.

And I need something fast, safe, and reliable to move around the islands in.

"I can go as high as fourteen-thousand-dollars. That's all I have."

Gentry stroked his gray-stubble chin. "Hmmm…you're talking cash money, right?"

"Yes. If I had more to spend, I would. I really love the boat."

Gentry's eyes narrowed as he considered the offer. "I believe you, young lady. And that does mean something to me. I'd like to see her go to someone who'll appreciate her. I've seen you out on the water. It was a few months ago. You were behind the wheel of a little runabout heading out of Roche Harbor. There was some chop out there, like today, but you were handling it just fine. Looked like you knew what you were doing."

Adele waited while Gentry continued to stroke his chin. He looked up and shrugged.

"I tell you what. Take her for a spin, and when you get back, if you still want her, we'll talk turkey."

Gentry held up a set of keys. "Here you go. She has plenty of fuel. Take her out, don't be afraid to run her hard, and when you get back, I'll be here waiting."

"You sure?"

Gentry nodded. "Absolutely. Every boat has something unique to say, but the only time you can truly hear it is on the water. So, take her out and see if you enjoy the conversation."

"Don't you want to come too?"

"Nah, I trust you."

Adele took the keys and stepped onto the boat. Though only a foot wider and six feet longer than Decklan's runabout, the Chris Craft felt huge by comparison. She sat down at the helm and turned the ignition. After a few rotations, the diesel fired up and then settled into a low, gurgling idle.

"You ready?" Gentry asked.

Adele nodded and Gentry untied. Adele bumped the throttle into reverse and was impressed by how quickly the boat reacted. It moved backward in a perfectly straight line. Once fully out of the slip, she put the boat into forward gear, turned the wheel, and then glanced back at the dock. Gentry gave her a thumbs up.

"Nicely done. Enjoy yourself out there! I think you two are going to get along just fine."

The waters outside Friday Harbor were a bit more agitated than Adele had anticipated. A stiff breeze blowing from the west combined with a strong tidal change had created rows of white caps that broke across the entirety of San Juan Channel that separated the much larger San Juan Island from nearby Shaw Island.

Adele pointed the Chris Craft into the waves and pushed down on the throttle until the tachometer registered 1800 rpm. The bow lifted for a few seconds and then lowered as the Lancer settled into a comfortable cruising speed. Adele was amazed at how the boat shrugged off the waters smacking up against its hull. Just as Gentry had promised, it easily cut through the waves as if they were hardly there. The GPS indicated the boat was doing eighteen knots, a remarkable pace given the conditions.

Soon the Lancer was speeding toward Shaw, a five-thousand-acre island with fewer than three-hundred residents. It was also home to a group of Benedictine nuns who lived at a remote monastery near the center of the island that was completely independent from the outside world. Shaw was the smallest of the four primary San Juan Islands and as such, often overlooked by passing tourists. The locals knew better, though. Its shores offered ample fishing grounds while the flat interior and abundance of old-growth trees made it a favorite among bicyclists and hikers.

The only commercial enterprise was the general store directly across from the ferry terminal. Next to the store was a little wooden kiosk where locals left notes for island neighbors to pick up. That way they didn't have to wait for the often island-slow postal service. It was the absence of commercialism that had long made Shaw among the most secretive of the islands which, in turn, lured some of the world's wealthiest to build vacation homes there, including a certain Seattle software developer.

Adele didn't care about vacationing billionaires, though. She was having her first conversation with the Chris Craft. The Lancer's bow continued to easily work through the oncoming waves. The steering was comfortably firm and precise.

A ferry moved down the channel on its way toward Friday Harbor. Adele watched its approach, noted the large wake its passing created, and decided to give the Chris Craft a tougher test. She made a wide circle, pointed toward the ferry wake, and accelerated.

The torque from the Lancer's engine pushed Adele back into the seat, a sensation which caused her to grin. The saltwater spray hit the windshield. The tach indicated 2200 rpm. The speed hovered around twenty-five knots. The waves attempted to push the bow off course, but Adele was able to easily keep the boat tracking straight. She looked up and saw rows of faces pressed up against the glass of the ferry ship's windows looking down at her. Normally small boats avoided ferry wakes. The ferry passengers were likely wondering why Adele was driving right into one.

A churning four-foot wave loomed ahead. Adele was an experienced enough boater to know how varied boat wakes could be. Smaller craft produced what many called "skinny" wakes that passed by quickly while larger vessels like the passing ferry created much larger but slower moving wakes that often appeared smaller from a distance than they actually were. That made them far more dangerous as they tended to catch the less experienced by surprise.

Normally Adele would have slowed her speed but not today. Gentry had urged her to run the Lancer hard. She was about to do just that.

Let's see what you're really made of.

The wake lifted the bow upward. Adele gripped the steering wheel tightly and braced for the impact that would immediately follow. The bow plunged down into the trough. Frothy green water pummeled the windshield. The Chris Craft's hull shuddered beneath Adele's feet. This was followed by a temporary calm as the Lancer sped across the water toward the wake on the opposite side of the ferry's path. This time Adele wasn't driving into the wake but chasing it, which presented a following sea – a far more difficult and dangerous challenge that would lift the boat's stern up while simultaneously pushing the bow down, making directional control almost impossible. This was the scenario that most often capsized lesser vessels and/or inexperienced captains. The trick was to accelerate as the boat rides the crest and then quickly decelerate while dropping off the wave to avoid smashing the front of the boat beneath the water.

In that situation, the amount of an engine's torque could be the difference between avoiding a watery catastrophe and creating one. The turbo diesel propelled the Lancer up the wake without complaint. When Adele quickly eased off the throttle, the bow dipped. There was a moment of panic when the wheel was almost yanked from Adele's grip as the back of the boat was pushed violently sideways. She gritted her teeth and kept the bow pointed straight. The engine didn't skip a beat. The Chris Craft again moved forward into calmer waters.

Adele pulled the throttle back into neutral and took a deep breath. The Lancer drifted slowly atop the waves. The wind had lessened. A few fat clouds that had earlier threatened rain passed by overhead leaving warm blue skies in their place. Adele ran her fingers along the fiberglass console. The Lancer had not merely met her expectations but had exceeded them.

A loud groan erupted directly behind the boat. Adele gasped after turning around to locate the source and discovered the round dark eyes of a massive male stellar sea lion staring back at her. The beast's golden-haired head bobbed up and down in the water. In the islands, a stellar sea lion sighting was nearly as rare as catching a pod of Orca Whales passing by. The males are four times the size of the more common harbor seal, often exceeding two thousand pounds. They sit atop the San Juan Islands sea life food chain with only the Orca to contend with.

Adele stood up and walked to the back of the boat with her camera phone at the ready. She was close enough she could count the long yellow whiskers growing out of the creature's white-gray snout. It was an old warrior with a face and neck marred by scars, proof of its many previous battles. To survive so long in the harsh watery world that was its home was a testament to the great sea lion's toughness.

After Adele took its picture, the sea lion arched its head back and bellowed. It was a proud and defiant gesture from an old king unwilling to relinquish its crown. It regarded Adele for a few more seconds before turning toward Shaw Island and slipping beneath the water's surface. In the distance, the ferry horn announced its arrival into Friday Harbor. Adele pushed the Lancer's throttle forward and made her way there as well.

Gentry stood waiting on the docks as promised. Adele returned the boat to its slip and tied up.

"Well, how'd she do for you?" Gentry asked.

Adele glanced at the Chris Craft and nodded. "It's just like you said, Mr. Pickett, rides true and takes the water as well as any twenty-three-footer could."

Gentry scowled. "What's this 'Mr. Pickett' stuff? You call me Gentry."

Adele grinned. "OK."

"So, you want to be the new owner?"

"I'd love to, but fourteen thousand is really all I have, and I doubt that's going to be enough."

Gentry chuckled. "In this life, something is worth what one is willing to pay, and another is willing to sell for. I'm pretty sure that's what the egg heads in their ivory towers call the free market. If you're the buyer, then I guess that means my boat is worth exactly fourteen-thousand dollars."

Adele's eyes widened. "Really? Are you sure?"

Gentry nodded. "Yeah, I'm sure. She's all yours. Enjoy."

Adele stammered her gratitude. "Uh, thank you. Really, I mean that. I love the boat – it's perfect. I'll need a little time to get you a cashier's check. If someone offers you more, you won't sell it out from under me, will you?"

Gentry stuck out his hand. "We'll shake on it. That's how things are done on the islands. Our word is our bond. When you're ready, bring the money by. I'm down here most days."

Adele's hand was swallowed up by Gentry's rough-calloused one. They shook, and Gentry nodded.

Gentry walked away, leaving Adele standing next to her new boat. Just-arrived tourists clogged the street above the marina, blissfully ignorant of the conflict that was brewing prior to that evening's council meeting. Part of Adele resented their ignorance. Life would be so much easier without the burden of knowing things others didn't.

With knowledge comes responsibility and for Adele that responsibility was to her friends and the people of the islands.

That meant going to war with Yuri Popov – a war with an uncertain and potentially very dangerous outcome.

Chapter 10

The Island Gazette

San Juan Island shooting leads to troubling questions
by Adele Plank

Sergei Kozlov, aged 39, was shot and killed by San Juan County Sheriff Lucas Pine last week. The shooting took place during the morning hours near the Friday Harbor business district. Initial reports indicate Mr. Kozlov stopped his vehicle in the middle of the street and then pointed a gun at Sheriff Pine. The sheriff ordered Kozlov to lower his weapon. When Kozlov refused the request, Sheriff Pine fired once. Kozlov was later declared dead at the scene.

An inquiry into the shooting was immediately initiated, headed by former Washington State patrolman, Dan Walser. In what some are calling a remarkable coincidence, Mr. Walser happened to be visiting Friday Harbor the day of the shooting. Sheriff Pine has been placed on paid administrative leave during the inquiry.

Kozlov was a semi-regular visitor to the islands. He had previous run-ins with island law enforcement, including a recent illegal weapons charge. He was also rumored to be linked to organized crime, namely with alleged Vancouver B.C. Russian crime boss, Yuri Popov.

That is where the story of last week's lethal shooting takes an even more troubling turn. This reporter saw Dan Walser and Yuri

Popov together first-hand shortly after the shooting. Walser has since denied having any relationship with Mr. Popov even as his investigative authority has broadened to include private citizens unrelated to the shooting itself. Just yesterday, the office of *The Island Gazette* was raided by Mr. Walser. Property, including computers and software that allow for publishing of physical editions of the paper, was seized. Members of the county council have so far refused to answer requests for clarification on this matter.

Just as interesting, is the below photograph of a 'Dan Walser for San Juan County Sheriff' sign that was recently placed alongside a street in Friday Harbor. Mr. Walser is on record denying any knowledge of the sign. That denial is understandable given the glaring conflict of interest were he to consider running for the very office he is now investigating.

A council meeting is scheduled for this evening. Citizens are urged to present their concerns to the council regarding this and other matters at that time.

The article worked. The islands buzzed with the news of Walser's investigation and his possible links to organized crime. Adele had been careful not to reveal everything she knew but just enough to apply community pressure on both Walser and the council.

The council chambers were filled to capacity. With all the bodies and the low ceiling, the heat and humidity were stifling. The doors were left open to bring in some much-needed fresh air as well as give the mass of people gathered outside a chance to hear what was being said. Adele sat between Suze and Tilda. Tilda was saving the two seats next to her. Right before the meeting started, Adele looked up at the unexpected arrival of Decklan and Calista Stone.

She turned toward Tilda. "You actually convinced Decklan to leave his island?"

Tilda smiled. "As you know, I can be *very* persuasive. Besides, I only had to convince Calista. Where she goes, Decklan follows."

Decklan looked uncomfortable while Calista appeared intrigued by the great gathering of community interest. Adele hugged them both, and then they sat down next to Tilda. The eyes of each member of the council darted about the chambers. They were nervous. Adele hoped that nervousness would lead to her being able to tell who among them was working with Yuri Popov.

Walser sat at the far right of the council table with Lucas's deputies, Chancee Smith and Gunther Fox. Walser's face was unreadable. He appeared to be looking at everything and nothing. Gunther, a retired Marine well known for his to-the-point demeanor was a much easier read. Adele noticed him repeatedly glaring at Walser while Chancee kept her head down most of the time.

Councilman Roger Wilcox gaveled the council table. His ruddy complexion was even redder than usual, and his forehead dripped with perspiration.

The audience went quiet. The meeting started.

Wilcox looked up, cleared his throat, and shifted in his chair. "We have quite a turnout tonight. I appreciate seeing so many friends and neighbors. Uh, there will be time for public comment shortly. I would ask that until then everyone remain patient as we conduct normal council business."

Adele heard a murmur behind her. She turned around and saw Action Five News reporter Marianne Rocha and her cameraman pushing their way through the crowd. Both of them stood against the wall. Marianne instructed the cameraman to take a shot of the audience. Councilman Wilcox's gavel cracked the table once again.

"We ask members of the media to please be quiet as well. Thank you."

Marianne smiled, nodded, and then straightened the especially tight skirt that outlined her long legs. Adele caught more than a few men admiring the reporter's shapely thighs.

Tilda frowned. "I don't know who that woman is, but I already don't like her."

Suze leaned toward Adele. "Where is Sheriff Pine?" she whispered.

Adele shrugged. "Probably at home. I don't think he wanted to a part of this."

"What about Samantha? I haven't heard from her."

Adele remembered Samantha was supposed to have given her a copy of the surveillance tape by now. She stood up and looked around the council chambers. Samantha wasn't there.

"I don't know where she is. As soon as the meeting is over, I'll call her."

The council reviewed the contents of the previous meeting's minutes and voted to approve them. Councilman Wilcox then opened the floor to comments from the public. The room went silent. Nobody came forward to speak. Adele worried everyone there just wanted to observe and not participate. She looked at Walser and found him leaning back in his chair with his chin jutting upward. He appeared far too confident for Adele's liking.

Councilman Wilcox cleared his throat. "Well, if there are no comments then—"

Suze stood up and pointed at Walser. "I'd like someone to explain how it is he just happened to be here on the day of the shooting."

Several others in the audience nodded their agreement. Councilwoman Sandra Plume held up both hands as she slowly shook her head from side to side. A lifelong resident of the islands, Sandra was well-liked and respected, known for saying little in public but often saying the most important things when she did. Her short, wide stature and jowly face reminded Adele of a Basset Hound.

"That information – in fact, *any* information regarding the ongoing investigation into the recent shooting – cannot be made available to the public at this time. This isn't the choice of the council. That's a matter of strict protocol, ladies and gentlemen. I'm sorry, but we cannot answer those kinds of questions."

"Why were you on the islands that day, Mr. Walser?" Suze bellowed. Adele had never seen the normally happy-go-lucky bookstore owner so angry and determined.

Again, Councilman Wilcox's gavel struck the table. "Suze, we need you to please state your full name and address for the record. Thank you."

Suze rolled her eyes. "Suzanne Blatt from just up the road."

A ripple of chuckles moved across the room. Suze stared at Walser.

"We deserve to know how the man who is now conducting the investigation into the shooting just so happened to be here in Friday Harbor on the same day that shooting occurred. None of us are stupid. That is one hell of a coincidence, and we deserve answers. And while I'm at it, why is Mr. Walser conducting raids against *The Island Gazette*? How long before he is doing the same to all the other businesses on the island? Are you three responsible for giving him the authority to do so?"

Someone shouted from outside how they deserved to know the truth. Several more inside the council chambers did the same. Suze had lit the spark. The community push-back against whatever Walser and his backers were planning was finally underway.

Beatrice Baker, the middle-aged owner of Beatrice Breads and a business neighbor of *The Island Gazette* stood up. She nervously adjusted the bottom of her light sweater, took a deep breath, gave her name and address, then asked a question which caused Walser's lips to purse.

"I saw the picture of the campaign sign – the one with Walser's name on it. How is it that the man investigating the current sheriff also wants to replace him? That can't be legal can it?"

Outraged shouts filled the council chambers. Wilcox repeatedly banged the gavel and demanded order. Then something unexpected happened.

Dan Walser stood up.

The room went silent.

Walser nodded.

"I get it. Sheriff Pine is one of you and if there's one thing I've already learned from my time here is how you all care for your own. That's a wonderful thing. It really is. And if the sheriff did nothing wrong, if he acted within the rules governing his duty as a law enforcement officer, then I assure you my investigation will reach that conclusion. But as the council has already indicated, I cannot, and I will not discuss the specifics of that investigation. You see, I am a man who follows the rules. That is what true justice requires. A man died on your streets. He was shot dead by an important member of this community. Any death deserves a thorough and thoughtful investigation. That is all I am doing, which is something I know every one of you here tonight would want done if it was someone you knew and cared for who had been killed."

Walser glanced at Adele. "As for the seizure of property at your local paper, I am again unable to disclose my reasons for doing so. What I *will* say is that most here tonight are likely well aware of how close certain representatives of that paper are to Sheriff Pine. If necessary, I'll leave it to a grand jury to explore the nature of that relationship further."

There was a collective gasp throughout the council chambers. Adele noted how Councilman Wilcox rocked back in his chair as his head snapped to the side to look at Walser. She also felt the eyes of the community now on her as they awaited her response to Walser's accusation and his threat of a grand jury investigation.

Adele gathered her thoughts and prepared to stand, but Decklan stood first. He clasped his hands in front of him. His voice was a low, almost-whisper.

"My name is Decklan Stone. I am here tonight with my wife, Calista. Many here know our story. If anyone has suffered terribly at the hands of abusive law enforcement, it has been us. The person who revealed that abuse and saved Calista's life is Adele Plank, reporter and co-owner of *The Island Gazette*. That is but one example of Ms. Plank's devotion to truth and helping those in need on these islands. If she has concerns about the investigation being headed up by this Mr. Walser, then so do I and so should all of you. I support Adele. I support her reporting, and I support her newspaper. Thank you."

Decklan's statement was followed by brief, respectful applause. Adele waited to see if anyone else was going to speak. Unfortunately, someone did.

It was Dan Walser. He had remained standing during Decklan's comments.

"Thank you, Mr. Stone. You're right. I do know the remarkable story of your wife's survival and discovery. I also know that it was a corrupt former sheriff of these islands who was the primary cause of your wife's abuse. All I am doing now is ensuring another sheriff isn't engaged in similar corruption which might endanger public safety. I would think you of all people would appreciate that."

Decklan's features darkened. Adele knew that signaled his annoyance which in turn meant trouble for Walser who had foolishly decided to engage in a war of words with a world-renowned writer.

"What I appreciate in this matter, Mr. Walser, is honesty. If the events tonight were a chapter in a book, you would be the double-edged villain. Whether you smile or grimace, the look in your eyes indicates the same thing – arrogant defiance. But defiance of what? You have all the makings of a dangerous interloper. You're quite comfortable speaking of corruption, aren't you? It seems the concept is a familiar one. Perhaps you are merely speaking of that which you know so well..."

Decklan paused. Heads leaned forward in anticipation of what he would say next.

"…as well as you know yourself."

Walser's jaw clenched. His overconfident wall had been breached.

"What are implying Mr. Stone? Why don't you drop the fancy words and come right out and say it, so I can turn around and sue you for slander?"

The threat of legal action caused most in the audience to shake their heads in disgust. The independent-minded island residents had a long-established natural aversion to third-party interests getting involved in things that could otherwise be settled by more direct and honorable means.

"Ah, there it is, the threat of a lawsuit – so often the scoundrel's last refuge."

Walser's cheeks burned crimson. His verbal balttle with Decklan was proving disastrous.

"I would ask the chair to please restore order. This back and forth between Mr. Walser and Mr. Stone is not pertinent to council business."

It was the first time since the council meeting had started that Councilman Joe Box said something. Box had had a head much like his name – large and square with a flat face and deep-set eyes. His hair was shaved close to the scalp. He spoke with a tone that indicated to Adele he wanted the meeting to be over as soon as possible.

"We all have lives to get back to, Mr. Chairman. Please wrap up the public comments so we can move on to our agenda items."

Tilda stood up. "Not before you tell all of us who was responsible for bringing Mr. Walser here. Whose idea was it to put him in charge of the inquiry?"

Wilcox cracked his gavel. "I'm sorry, Ms. Ashland, but you do not have the floor. Please sit down and be quiet."

Tilda's eyes blazed. "I'll sit down when you give me an answer, Roger. Stop using that damn gavel and start using your head! There is no council business more important than telling us the truth about what is *really* going on here. Lucas Pine has been a good sheriff. He deserves better than this. He certainly deserves better from the three of you. And as for that sweating tub of accusation called Walser sitting up there thinking he can intimidate me into looking away, I'm with Decklan. I don't trust him."

Councilman Wilcox began pounding his gavel again but then stopped as all three radios hanging from the belts of Walser, Gunther, and Chancee started to chirp. Seconds later everyone inside the council chambers heard the siren wail of the island's only ambulance.

Chancee brought her radio to her ear and then whispered something to Gunther who immediately moved toward the exit. When Walser moved to follow, Gunther spun around and put his hand on Walser's chest.

"No, I don't think so. You don't belong there. Not after what you did to them."

When Walser started to protest, Gunther stepped into him until they were nearly nose to nose. He spoke through clenched teeth.

"I said no."

The siren grew louder.

Adele felt her phone vibrate. She brought it out and looked down. It was a text from Samantha. The message was just two words.

Avery Jenkins

Chapter 11

Adele held Avery's hand. Bess sat on the other side of the hospital bed with her head resting on her husband's sunken chest.

Avery had fallen down an entire flight of stairs leaving him with a concussion and what island medical staff feared was a broken hip. A Medevac flight was scheduled to transport him from Friday Harbor to Harborview Medical Center in Seattle for further evaluation and treatment.

Bess sat up and wiped away tears. "He hasn't opened his eyes since I found him. I thought he was dead." Adele reached out and took Bess's hand.

"Avery is a lot stronger than he looks. He's going to get the best care possible at Harborview. The chopper will be here soon."

Bess gave Adele a grateful smile, but her eyes continued to reflect her uncertainty that things were actually going to be fine. "I need to use the bathroom."

Adele nodded. "Go ahead. I'll stay with him."

When the hospital room door opened, Adele saw a mass of people gathered in the reception area. It seemed all of Friday

Harbor was waiting to hear how Avery was doing – including Lucas.

Avery's hand flinched. His eyes partially opened. Adele intended to stand up so she could tell Bess, but Avery shook his head.

"No. Don't leave."

His eyes widened. He grimaced then looked down at the morphine drip going into his arm.

"I see they have me on the good stuff."

Adele smiled. "That they do.

Avery looked around. "Where am I?"

"You're still in Friday Harbor. They're transporting you to Harborview."

Avery tried to sit up. Adele gently held him down.

"Don't move. You hurt your hip and took quite a knock to the head."

"Did you say Harborview?"

"That's right."

Avery's body went limp. His eyes closed.

"Damn. I know what that means. I broke my hip, didn't I?"

"Possibly, yes."

Avery shook his head. "That's a death sentence for a man my age. I've seen the statistics."

"Don't talk like that. Bess needs you to be strong."

Avery sighed. "I know. I'll try."

Bess opened the door. She gasped when she realized Avery was conscious.

"Thank goodness you're awake!"

The couple hugged. Avery cried out in pain. Bess recoiled, clearly horrified that she might have hurt him.

"Should I get a doctor?" Adele asked.

Avery winced then shook his head. "No, I'm just sore is all. Like an elephant is sitting on my chest. Everything else feels fine. Maybe my hip is OK?"

Bess started to cry again. Avery pulled her toward him.

"There now, no need for that. I'm right here."

Bess gripped Avery's hands. "When I found you, I thought you were gone. All those stairs – it's a long fall. What happened? Did you just slip?"

Avery frowned. "I was outside the office. There was a smell in the air like, uh, lavender. It was quite strong. I heard a noise behind me, and then…that's all I recall. I woke up here."

"Were you pushed?" Adele asked.

Avery shrugged. "Pushed? Who would do that? *Why* would they do that?"

Adele and Bess looked at each other. Bess's eyes narrowed, and her mouth tightened.

"That damn Walser is who. Our online edition comes out the same day you're pushed down a flight of stairs? Coincidence? I think not."

Adele frowned. "Walser was at the council meeting, though. It couldn't have been him."

Avery groaned. Bess crouched over him.

"What is it?"

Avery closed his eyes tight and gritted his teeth. He was having trouble breathing. Adele was about to get a doctor when the door opened, and Lucas stepped inside.

"The Medivac is almost here. We're about to move Mr. Jenkins to the airport for the transfer."

Bess cried out. "Something's wrong! Please help!"

Avery's eyes rolled up into the back of his head. His bone-thin fingers extended out at his sides like claws. Lucas yelled for a doctor. Two nurses ran into the room. The older of the two requested everyone wait outside.

Bess clung to Avery's hand. "What's going on? Someone please tell me what's happening."

A nurse guided Bess away from the bed. Adele wrapped an arm around her shoulders. A tall, gray-haired doctor came in, saw Avery, and immediately called for a crash cart. He pointed at Lucas.

"Sheriff, these people need to go – now."

Bess pleaded with the doctor. "You save him, you hear me! This isn't his time, and I'm not ready to be alone."

A nurse helped Adele to move Bess into the reception area. Just beyond the door, Bess's knees buckled. She started to sob but then looked up at all the faces of friends and neighbors in the room with her and immediately straightened her shoulders and wiped away her tears.

Bess accepted hugs and assurances that Avery was in good hands even as nurses continued to scramble in and out of the hospital room. Though the door was closed, Adele could hear the doctor shouting instructions.

"Clear!"

The doctor's voice rang out again.

"Clear!"

Adele helped Bess to sit down. The reception room went quiet. Twenty minutes passed before the doctor came back out and stood before them. He was out of breath and sweating. Bess leaned against Adele for support as she stood up.

The doctor motioned for Lucas. The two walked together into an adjoining hallway. Adele could hear the doctor saying something but couldn't make out the words. Lucas nodded and then spoke into his radio. His face was grim. He avoided looking at anyone else in the room. Adele felt Bess's hand tighten around her forearm.

"What's the sheriff doing, Adele? Who is he talking to?"

Adele started to cry. She knew Lucas had just canceled the Medivac flight.

Avery Jenkins was dead.

The doctor walked up to Bess. "I am so sorry, Mrs. Jenkins. It appears to have been a massive heart attack. We tried everything we could, but your husband is gone."

Bess made a sound like she had been kicked in the stomach. Her mouth trembled. She looked down.

"I understand. Thank you, Doctor. Can I see him?"

The doctor nodded. "Of course."

Bess whispered to Adele. "Don't let me fall."

Adele held her close. "I've got you."

The two walked arm-in-arm back into the room. The door closed behind them. The sound made Adele flinch. It reminded her of a tomb. A nurse stepped away from the bed to reveal Avery's body. His eyes were closed. Bess began to sob. She started to fall forward. Adele held her up.

Bess stroked the little bit of hair that remained on Avery's head. "It's been you and me for so long I don't know what I'm to do without you. You were the most wonderful, honorable, stubborn old fool. We talked and loved and fought for years and years and years. Everything I am I was with you. You always said you would go first and isn't it just like you to have to keep your word."

Bess kissed Avery's forehead. "You wait for me, Avery Jenkins. When it's my time, yours better be the first face I see, or it'll be another argument. You hear me?"

Adele dabbed away tears. Bess stood up and shook her head. "It doesn't seem real, does it? My Avery is gone."

Adele felt the same. Avery's passing was surreal. He lay there as if he was merely asleep. He had done so much to give Adele her life on the islands.

Bess cleared her throat. Some of her familiar toughness had returned.

"He said he heard something behind him right before he fell. I know Walser was at the council meeting, but I also know if someone did push Avery, Walser is involved. I feel it in my bones."

Adele had already been replaying Avery's words in her mind.

I was outside the office. There was a smell in the air like, uh, lavender. It was quite pronounced. I heard a noise behind me, and then…that's all I recall. I woke up here.

A noise and the smell of lavender. It wasn't much to go on.

Bess took a deep breath and turned around. "There are a lot of people out there who respected my husband. Good manners demand I thank them for being here."

Adele followed Bess into the reception room. Many promised to help Bess with anything she might need in the coming days and weeks. Lucas was one of the last to give Bess his condolences. Bess gripped his muscular arms tightly as she looked up at him.

"Promise me you'll help us find who pushed Avery down those stairs."

Lucas glanced at Adele.

"What?"

Before Adele could explain, the hospital's glass entrance doors parted, and Dan Walser walked in. He scanned the room and then pointed at Lucas.

"I need to speak with you, Mr. Pine. It seems you were in violation of the conditions of your administrative leave tonight. Now I'm sorry to hear Mr. Jenkins was injured but rules are rules, and you don't seem to be willing to follow them."

"*He* was involved," Bess hissed.

Lucas peered down at Bess and then tipped his head toward Walser. "You think he had something to do with what happened to Avery?"

Bess glared at Walser as she nodded. "You're damn right I do, Sheriff."

"I'm talking to you, Mr. Pine!" Walser bellowed. Adele noted how Walser didn't afford Lucas the title of sheriff when addressing him. All eyes in the room turned toward Lucas. Everyone was curious to see how he would respond. Gunther Fox positioned himself between Walser and Lucas.

"He's baiting you, Sheriff. Just ignore him. Everyone here is on your side."

Lucas glowered at Walser. "I know. He's pathetic."

Adele was relieved to see Lucas keep his composure. He gently gripped Bess's upper arms.

"Bess, I promise I'll conduct a thorough investigation into what happened to Avery."

Bess fought back tears. "Thank you, Sheriff. I know you will."

A hand clamped down on Lucas's shoulder. "That investigation will have to wait, Mr. Pine. You aren't the sheriff anymore, remember?"

Lucas whirled around and stared down at Walser. Adele pulled Bess back, not wanting her to get hurt.

"This isn't the time for this. A man just died," Lucas seethed.

Walser's mouth fell open. "Oh, I didn't know Mr. Jenkins had passed away. I'm sorry for your loss Mrs. Jenkins."

Walser stared up at Lucas. "I still have a job to do, though. Mr. Pine did you or did you not respond to the emergency dispatch involving Mr. Jenkins tonight?"

Adele could feel the brewing storm inside of Lucas as he slowly clenched his fists at his sides.

"I did. Someone was hurt. I went to assist."

Walser shook his head. "Well, you see that there is a problem. You're not allowed to be doing that. You're on leave pending what remains an ongoing investigation. Your refusal to follow the rules puts the county at risk. We can't have you running around pretending you're still the sheriff because as you know – *you're not.* I have no choice but to formally suspend you."

Gunther pointed at Walser. "Who the hell do you think you are? The sheriff was just helping out!"

"Your support of Mr. Pine's non-compliance is duly noted, Deputy Fox. Perhaps I need to consider including you in the scope of my investigation."

Gunther muttered a profanity and Lucas let out a low, rumbling growl. Adele knew that meant he had reached the limits of his patience. The storm had arrived and all there was left to do was to take cover.

Lucas reached out and grasped Walser by the collar. A panicked Gunther tried to hold the sheriff back. Lucas pushed Walser backward while dragging Gunther along with him. Thick veins looked like they might erupt from beneath the skin of Lucas's arms. Walser demanded he be let go. Lucas ignored him. People scrambled to get out of the way and clear a path to the exit. Walser grunted and strained to break from Lucas's grip but couldn't.

An exhausted Gunther gave up trying to stop the sheriff and let Lucas go. He put his hands on his hips and shook his head.

"Damn, that boy is strong."

The sliding door opened. Lucas spun Walser around and grabbed the back of his collar with one hand and took hold of his belt with the other. Walser screeched his outrage.

"Let go of me!"

"I intend to," Lucas snarled.

Adele watched in stunned admiration as Lucas lifted Walser completely off the ground and then flung him like a side of beef through the open doorway. Walser's hands made little circular motions in the air like he was trying to fly. He didn't fly, though. Instead, he struck the pavement with a loud grunt. It took a few seconds for Walser to catch his breath. He stood up on unsteady feet, put one hand on the butt of his gun and wagged a finger at Lucas with the other.

"Well, you just did it. I think it's safe to say that as far as you serving as this community's sheriff, those days are definitely over. I'm pressing charges. You just assaulted me."

Lucas stepped toward Walser. Gunther again struggled to hold him back.

"He's not worth it, Sheriff. Let him threaten all he wants. I saw what really happened."

Gunther looked around. "We *all* did."

The smile fell from Walser's face. "What are you talking about Deputy?"

Gunther shrugged. "It's really pretty simple. You showed up here at a time of extreme stress not only for Mrs. Jenkins but everyone else who knew her husband. You started shouting. Some might even describe it as a verbal assault. In fact, I'm tempted to give you a sobriety test right here and now. Mr. Walser, are you currently under the influence of drugs or alcohol?"

Walser was so upset his cheeks quivered when he spoke. "You think you can intimidate me? You really believe these people will go along with your version of events?"

Bess Jenkins stepped forward. "I will."

Suze reached down and held Bess's hand. "Me too."

Samantha and Chancee were next to voice their support for Gunther and Lucas. They were then joined by every other person in the reception room, including the doctor.

Dan Walser stood alone. He appeared to want to say more. Lucas stood in the doorway staring at him but said nothing. The two men locked eyes. Walser looked away first. He turned and left.

Lucas shook Gunther's hand. "Thanks."

Gunther grunted. "I know his kind all too well after years in the military taking orders from useless turds just like him. A guy like that wouldn't last ten minutes in battle. They'd rather turn tail and run - just like he did tonight."

Lucas sighed. "He might have run away, but I'm certain he'll be circling back."

Gunther didn't appear too concerned. "Fine, when he does, we'll be ready."

Bess started to laugh and cry at the same time. When she noticed everyone was looking at her, she shook her head.

"Avery would have loved to have seen what just happened. He was always a fight-the-power sort. And Sheriff Pine, I have never witnessed something so wonderful as when you threw that man out of here and believe me when I say I'd pay good money to watch you do it again!"

There were more tears, laughter, and hugs all around. Adele watched how gentle Lucas was with Bess and how Bess clung to him like a lost ship seeking safe passage through what were terribly troubled, emotional waters. Lucas had recently buried his father. Bess would now be doing the same for her husband. Lucas was young, tall, and strong. Bess was old, short, and frail, yet at that moment, both were far more similar than different.

Adele looked over at the room that contained Avery's body. He was gone, but in the moments that immediately followed his passing, he remained as alive as ever in the hearts of those who had called him husband, colleague, and friend.

She would miss him terribly.

Chapter 12

The day after Avery's passing Adele spent the morning checking in on Bess. By the time Adele was getting ready to leave, Suze had shown up as well to see how Bess was doing. She stopped Adele outside and handed her a flash drive.

"Samantha gave it to me. She hasn't had a chance to check the footage herself yet. She's certain Walser is on to her. The poor thing is scared to death."

That had been an hour ago. Adele was now on the water in the Chris Craft Lancer she purchased from Gentry. She brought payment to him, and he gave her the title and keys. The boat was officially hers and speeding toward that day's destination – Rosario. The trip was a welcome reprieve from the painful void left by Avery's passing. There would come a time when she would stop and more fully process his death. For now, though, she had work to do.

Adele was still learning the Chris Craft's limitations and finding they were few. It swallowed up the watery chop like a Cadillac absorbing bumps in the road. Though even faster than Decklan's outboard-powered runabout, the Lancer's ride was smoother. What impressed Adele the most was how well it steered. Over-correction was a common problem with smaller craft, especially those being captained by a less-experienced hand. Unlike cars, which respond immediately due to driving on a permanent and unmoving surface, all boats present their drivers with constantly changing conditions that require subtle, or sometimes more aggressive, changes in direction and speed. The Chris Craft still required such corrections, but it did so in a far more forgiving manner that Adele was quick to appreciate.

The boat felt right.

She passed a slow-moving trawler. The captain waved. Adele waved back - a common courtesy among boaters in the San Juans. It was just a few minutes later that Adele pulled up alongside the Rosario marina guest dock. She tied off the Chris Craft and walked up the hill to the resort.

The reception area was all class and smiles. Adele introduced herself and informed the sharp-dressed young woman behind the check-in counter that she was there to meet with a guest named Vincent Weber. The woman typed in the name, glanced at the computer monitor and then nodded.

"Mr. Weber is currently on the veranda. Right this way, please."

The short walk to the veranda surrounded Adele in the resort's mix of dark wood, white pillars, and stone. She still found it hard to believe that the massive structure was once a private residence. The woman led Adele back outside and motioned toward a small table overlooking the waters of East Sound.

"Mr. Weber is expecting you. Please enjoy your time here at Rosario."

Vincent looked up from his drink and waved Adele over.

"There you are, Ms. Plank. I received the message you wished to see me. Have a seat. They make the most amazing concoction here called the "Low Tide." It's a mix of gin, pear-brandy, a touch of jasmine, and wait for it . . . local seaweed! Can you imagine? I'm already on my third!"

It was still early afternoon, and Vincent was already well on his way to being drunk. Adele was sure he hadn't shaved since arriving at the islands, and by the look of his badly wrinkled shirt, she wondered if he no longer considered fresh laundry a necessity either.

Vincent lifted his arms up and grinned. "Quite a location for the movie, don't you think? This place is amazing. I've never felt so relaxed. It's as if all the pressures of working in Hollywood have fallen away. I now understand why you love it here so much."

Adele noted other hotel guests glancing at Vincent. He was speaking loudly, and his words were slurred.

"It's certainly beautiful," she answered.

Vincent took a long sip and then stared up at the cloudless sky. "It's more than that – it's magical. I can feel it. There's energy all around us. The house, the property, the water, the cliffs – it's all in perfect harmony. That is why Rosario will be the writer character's home. This will be the primary location for the film. My instincts were right."

Vincent held up his drink and gave Adele a glassy-eyed grin. "As they so often are."

Adele shook her head. "But this isn't anything like Decklan's home. He lives on his own little island. It's remote, private – like him. You're changing everything about who he really is."

Vincent tapped his temple. "Artistic license. My film is to be inspired by Decklan and Calista's story, not shackled to it. My vision will be an improvement."

"An improvement? Really? Have you bothered to tell *them* that?"

Vincent rolled his eyes. "Bah! You're quibbling details at me. If it's what I want, it's what I'll get because in the end it's what's best for the film and that's all that matters. Besides, you don't want to see the project delayed or worst yet, shelved. You still have a nice fat studio check coming to you."

"If your film doesn't have Decklan and Calista's support, it won't have mine. I could care less about the money, Mr. Weber."

Vincent wagged a finger at Adele. "That's a lie. Sure, it sounds noble. Remember, I'm from Hollywood. I'm drowning in fabricated noble intentions but believe me, at the end of the day, *everyone* is killing each other over money because the cliché is true. Money is power. The kind of power that allows one to tell the world you don't give a damn because you don't have to."

Adele recalled Roland once telling her something very similar. She didn't like thinking of him and Vincent Weber sharing a common philosophy.

"That's not the world I choose to live in."

Vincent chuckled. "You poor thing, you actually think *choice* is involved? The studio isn't paying for my trip here, my room, my food, my drink - none of this is being done so I might create art. No, I'm here to ensure a profit. My job is to create a story the studio can then sell to producers willing to put up the cash to make a film version happen."

"I thought you *were* an artist. Your screenplay was amazing."

Vincent finished the last of his drink and signaled for another. "Of course it's amazing. I wrote it. The purpose of that screenplay was to take my career to the next level. I've done the indie film stuff. I've made a little money, but I want more. I want everything, and I intend to get it. That's why I'm here in this place at this time. I'm creating my everything moment. And you're part of it, Adele. How exciting for you!"

For Adele, excitement wasn't the word that came to mind. Vincent was a train wreck. Another drink was put in front of him. He took a sip and grinned.

"Mmmm…breakfast, lunch, and dinner."

Vincent suddenly looked up at Adele as if he was seeing her for the first time. His focused on her face as he cocked his head.

"I forgot you came here to ask me something. What is it?"

Adele leaned forward and lowered her voice. "Has a man named Dan Walser been here to see you?"

Vincent shook his head. "No, never heard of him. Why?"

"It's island stuff – political. If he does contact you, please let me know."

"Ah, a bit of island intrigue is it? Why would this Dan Walser want to see me?"

"I'm not sure."

Vincent shrugged. "Well, if he wants to find me, this is where I'll be for the next few days. Oh! Have I told you the new title?"

"Title for what?"

Vincent took another drink. "The film, I'm calling it *Rosario's Revenge.*"

"What happened to calling it *The Writer*?"

"I recently met with a potential foreign investor for the project. She thought the title should reflect a story with more action and suspense. She was so impressed by the resort she suggested *Rosario's Revenge*. I agreed. It's a good title."

Adele didn't hide her disapproval. "Decklan and Calista's story isn't about revenge. It's about love and survival overcoming years of painful isolation and guilt."

Vincent's tone was hard and dismissive. "It's *my* project, Ms. Plank. My film. My reputation. If I wanted your input, I would have asked for it. I didn't."

"It's not my input you need to worry about. There's no way Decklan and Calista will agree to this. I'm seeing them after I leave here. They're going to know what you plan to do."

Vincent pouted. It made him look like a drunken child in need of a shave and a shower.

"I don't respond to threats."

Adele had run out of patience. Being with Vincent Weber felt too much like babysitting. She had asked him about Walser, and he gave his answer. It was time to go.

"Like I said, I'll be telling them your plans for the film. Don't expect them to be supportive of the changes. That's between you and them, though. In the meantime, remember to let me know if Walser reaches out to you. Don't forget. It's important."

Vincent raised his glass. "I promise. Until then – I drink."

Adele was happy to leave Vincent to his alcohol haze. She was looking forward to visiting more with Decklan and Calista at their island home. She walked past the Rosario Resort reception desk and then stopped when she suddenly recalled something Vincent had said.

I recently met with a potential foreign investor for the project. She thought the title should reflect a story with more action and suspense.

Adele returned to Vincent's table. He looked up and frowned.

"What is it?"

Adele remained standing. She remembered the description Samantha gave of the woman whose unscheduled arrival at the Sheriff's Office had made Walser so nervous.

"The foreign investor you mentioned. Was she Russian?"

Vincent's head snapped back like he had been slapped. "How in the hell did you know that?"

His reaction gave Adele her answer.

"What was her name?" she asked.

Vincent scowled. He rubbed his bloodshot eyes and wobbled on his chair. Adele waited.

"Do you know her? Is there a problem?"

"There could be. I need her name."

Vincent took a long sip and then stared at Adele with narrowed eyes. "You ever consider acting? You have a real girl-next-door quality about you. The brown hair, a pleasant face – I might be able to use you."

Adele ignored the offer. "Just tell me the woman's name."

"Only if you promise to do something for me."

"What is it?"

Vincent swirled what little was left of his drink. "You have to promise not to tell Decklan and Calista about the changes to the film. Let me be the one to inform them."

"Will you actually do it?"

Vincent sighed. His slurring was getting worse.

"Of course. I gave you my word."

"Fine, I won't say anything to them – for now."

Vincent grinned. "Thank you."

Adele watched him start to nod off. She cleared her throat. "The woman's name?"

Vincent opened his eyes. "She introduced herself as Liya Vasa."

"How did she know you were here?"

Vincent shrugged. "I don't know. I don't care. She arrived, asked me questions about the film, its profit potential, and how much I needed to get it going. I told her. We had a nice talk and she promised to get back to me. That's it. Now if you don't mind, I would like to get back to my drink."

Adele didn't mind. She had a name. That's all she had come there for.

"Goodbye, Mr. Weber."

Vincent's eyes were again closed. He mumbled his reply.

"Goodbye, Ms. Plank. Oh, and give that acting thing some thought. The world could use a nice face like yours."

"Yeah, I'll do that."

Adele left Rosario. She was eager to be back on the water and away from Vincent and the stink of Hollywood insecurity and self-importance that swirled around him.

Chapter 13

It was the following morning when Adele parked the Chris Craft next to her sailboat in Roche Harbor for the first time. It was a tight fit, but she managed. Though she had enjoyed the overnight stay with Decklan and Calista, her mind was already racing with the details of what she intended to do next.

That intent would require some help from Bob Tinnis, the Customs Officer Adele had come to know last winter. Tinnis had proven he wasn't always a by-the-book guy and that was what Adele needed because her plan required her to be as "off-the-books" as possible.

"Sure, I can do that. It's not a problem as long as it doesn't involve anything illegal. It's a simple reporting delay - happens all the time. Besides, I'm almost retired. I don't really give a damn. Plus, I have a guy on the Canadian side who owes me. I can have him delay the report for both your arrival and departure from Canada. I won't even ask what you're up to but if you decided you wanted to tell me I wouldn't mind."

Adele was pleased to see that the sixty-something Bob was in far better shape than he had been just a few months earlier. He had lost some weight. His eyes were clear. The thick gray head of hair had a bit of shine to it. He appeared healthy and in good spirits.

"It involves what happened to Sergei Kozlov."

Bob stroked his mustache. "I hate to state the obvious but Kozlov is dead and our mutual friend the sheriff was the one who shot him. Does this have something to do with the investigation into the shooting? I have to admit I'm surprised that hasn't been wrapped up already. It seems like a clear case of self-defense on Lucas's part."

Adele considered telling Bob her entire plan but decided it was best to keep as much of what she was doing a secret. "Yeah, it's related to that."

"And you think there are answers to be found in Vancouver?"

"I'm not sure."

Bob frowned. "You better be careful, Adele. If my hunch is right, your plan is to go poking around Yuri Popov's backyard. I don't think he'll appreciate that."

"If everything goes as planned I'll be in and out of there without him even knowing."

"My guess is you're going whether or not I think you should."

Adele nodded. "That's true, but your help would make it a whole lot easier."

"I'm happy to help, but I'm also worried you're biting off more than you can chew."

"People have been telling me that since I came to these islands. I'm still here. I'll be fine."

Bob sighed. "OK, here's the deal. You're already set up with a NEXUS card, right?"

Adele nodded. "Yeah, I've had one since college, so I didn't have to wait in those long lines to get across the border."

"Your NEXUS privileges make it pretty simple. Three hours after you leave here I'll call it into my border security contact in Canada. That will allow you to come and go as you please up there for about twenty-four hours. I will need to let him know what your port of entry will be, though."

"How did you know I was going by boat?"

Bob chuckled. "I saw you come in on that Chris Craft this morning. That's a sweet ride. If you want to get in and out quick, that's the way to do it. You likely already know that. Just make sure you're not transporting any contraband – weapons, drugs, etc. If you're stopped and searched, and have anything like that in your possession, it would be my ass, and I'd rather not lose what little pension I have coming to me when I retire."

"No – it'll just be me. I'm going to Vancouver."

"Good. Then what you do now is wait until early evening – around six o'clock. There's a one-hour window at that time when border security changes shifts. The ones working the end of the shift are ready to go home. The ones showing up need time to get acclimated and normally they're in no hurry to do so. Right before six you leave here and haul ass. If water conditions allow, you'll be to Vancouver before dark. If not, you might have to chug along at night. If that happens, you damn well better take your time.

"When you leave Roche, point your bow toward the west side of Stuart Island. That'll take you across the border into Canadian waters and the Gulf Islands. From there, it's a short shot between North Pender Island and Prevost Island. Those are protected waters. Even in bad weather, you should be able to make good time. Follow the entire length of Galiano Island and then turn east between Galiano and Valdes. This is where you'll be crossing big water – the Strait of Georgia. Respect those waters, Adele. Wear a life vest. If you need to, take it slow. And if you get into some trouble, swallow your pride, get on the radio, and call for help.

"You'll be way out there on the Strait and barely able to see any shoreline for a while. Pull up Wreck Beach on your GPS and trust there's land ahead. Once you pass Wreck Beach, hang a right into Vancouver. There's a marina in Granville Island which sits just underneath the Granville Bridge. It gets lots of visitors, especially this time of year. A little boat like yours will blend right into the crowd. Vancouver is a big city. You shouldn't be noticed. From there you can take a cab anywhere in the city you need to go."

Adele shook Bob's hand. "Thank you. I really appreciate the help."

Bob nodded. "You just make it back here in the same condition you're leaving, OK? Anything happens to you, and your readers will never forgive me. The last thing I need is to be on the wrong side of someone like Tilda Ashland or Lucas Pine. When will you be back?"

Adele quickly did the math in her head. "It shouldn't be any later than tomorrow afternoon."

Bob pointed at Adele. "I'm going to hold you to that, young lady."

Adele left the Customs Office, returned to her sailboat, and lay down to rest. Just before six she got up and hopped into the Chris Craft carrying a backpack of drinking water, granola bars, and a change of clothes. After fueling up the boat with fresh diesel and checking over her navigation equipment and the weather report, Adele idled out of Roche Harbor.

By six-thirty, she was blasting past Stuart Island on her way across the international border. A quick glance at the GPS marked the moment when she entered Canadian waters. North Pender Island was straight ahead. There was hardly any wind. While not glass smooth, the water's chop was less than a foot. It was easy going.

Adele had never been to the Gulf Islands before. Though smaller than the San Juans, they had a similarly rugged blend of dark rock and tall evergreen trees.

It took just over an hour to move past Pender and into the Trincomali Channel which ran the length of the narrow, seventeen-mile-long Galiano Island. The channel was a busy mix of fishing and cruising boat traffic. The water chop dissipated. Adele throttled up and was soon heading north along the Galiano shoreline at thirty knots.

The comfortable conditions continued even as Adele steered the Lancer between Galiano and Valdez islands and into the Strait of Georgia where slow-moving swells gently lifted and lowered the Chris Craft as it crossed the open water. After an hour of up and down driving, Adele glanced back and could barely make out the outline of the Gulf Islands. In front of her, the great mountains of British Columbia were still just little dark bumps on the horizon. There were no other boats around her. Adele was truly alone.

She looked down and found her knuckles were white where she gripped the steering wheel tightly. It wasn't so much from fear that made her do so but excitement and a strong sense of exploration. She was doing something she had never done before in a place she had never been.

The passing water blended with the drone of the Lancer's motor. The bow rose, fell, and then rose again, each motion both an end and a new beginning. The day's light was nearly gone. The lights of Vancouver could be seen in the distance. The GPS's depth-sounder indicated Adele was passing over an underwater ravine that was more than six hundred feet deep. It was an entire world beyond her own, yet linked by the same waters she now traveled across.

She was reminded of a quote by Sylvia Earl, a woman who had spent all of her current eighty-two-years of life exploring the sea.

Every time I slip into the ocean, it's like going home. I find the lure of the unknown irresistible.

Despite being alone surrounded by all that water and not knowing what the next few hours, days or weeks might hold, Adele had never felt more content and determined to find out. That was the lure of the water for her. When she was at sea, it presented the irresistible unknown and a repeating sense of coming home. On land was where she lived but on the water was where she felt the most alive.

With darkness came larger swells. The Chris Craft handled them beautifully and never felt off balance. There were a few times the bow dipped a foot or two below the water's surface after cresting the largest of the swells, but it quickly corrected and charged forward as the water ran off the sides of the hull leaving the cockpit completely dry. Adele was intensely focused but never worried. She was confident in the Lancer's ability to get her there and back in safety and comfort.

The last of the day had given way to night as the moon and stars watched over Adele from above. The Chris Craft climbed a swell, fell down the other side, and then went on to the next as the lights of Vancouver drew closer.

Adele took out her phone, plugged it into the stereo and turned it on. After glancing down to scroll through her playlist, she settled on Colin Hay's "Beautiful World", and turned up the volume until the music and her singing drowned out the sound of the engine and the water hitting the hull.

My-my-my it's a beautiful world.
I like swimming in the sea.
I like to go out beyond the white breakers.
Where a man can still be free.
Or a woman if you are one.
I like swimming in the sea.

It *was* a beautiful world. Adele was more convinced of that than she had ever been. She sang for Avery, Dr. Edmund Pine, Delroy Hicks, and all the others who had helped her to realize such beauty while coming into her life and then leaving it like the ebb and flow of the eternal tide.

Adele would always be grateful.

She would never forget.

Chapter 14

I'm not in Kansas anymore.

The monolithic mass of concrete above Adele's head signified a world far different than the laid-back simplicity of the San Juan Islands. Vancouver B.C. was a big city, home to more than a half-million people and one Adele considered her favorite on the North American West Coast. It had an undeniable European flavor to it, a byproduct of its beginnings as an extension of the former British Empire.

A procession of moving vehicles going back and forth over the Granville Bridge rumbled over Adele's head. Skyscrapers rose up like silent sentinels just beyond the shoreline.

A path led from the marina to the street above. Adele took the steps two at a time until she emerged on a paved sidewalk that extended from one end of the bridge to the other. She used her cell phone to pull up several taxi companies and called the first one listed and then worked her way down the list until the call was answered by a female dispatcher with a heavy Russian accent speaking broken English.

Adele ordered a cab and waited. It arrived within minutes and pulled to the side of the road. A short, bald, heavy-set man got out and opened the back door for Adele. Like the dispatcher he too was Russian.

"Where you want to go?"

"To the nearest bar owned by Yuri Popov."

The taxi driver did a double-take as he stood next to the open door. "What?"

Adele sat down in the backseat and repeated her instructions. "To the nearest bar owned by Yuri Popov."

The driver mumbled something, dropped behind the steering wheel with a grunt, and slammed the driver door shut. He glanced at Adele in the rearview mirror. The taxi smelled of sweat, Windex, fried food, and vomit.

"Who is this, uh, Yuri Popov?"

Adele knew the driver was playing dumb. "Yuri Popov, the gangster. I'm sure you've heard of him. Just take me to one of his bars. I'll pay double your normal rate."

The driver turned around so he could look at Adele directly. "What? Just because I'm Russian, you think I know some Russian gangster? Besides, why do you want to go to a place like that?"

Adele took out her phone. "If you can't take me, I'll just call another driver who will."

The driver shook his head. "Wait, wait, wait. I take you. You pay double, yes?"

Adele nodded. "That's what I said. Just make sure it's a bar owned by Popov, OK?"

The man nodded. "Yes, I do this for you. Perhaps I know a place."

The taxi's rear tires chirped as it accelerated onto the street and drove across the Granville Bridge. The driver continued to sneak looks at Adele in the rearview mirror.

"You know Yuri Popov?" he asked.

"I know he's an important man in the city."

The driver frowned. "Important? Perhaps. Dangerous? Definitely."

Adele saw a sign that said, "Welcome to Gastown." The brick sidewalks were full of fashionably-dressed men and women moving into and out of brightly-lit urban-chic boutique shops. High-end cars filled cobblestone streets lined with illuminated vintage lamp posts. It was old world meets new – a neighborhood whose people reminded Adele of well-dressed bees happily buzzing about with faces lit by electronic phone screens and eyes crackling from repeated doses of dark-bean caffeine.

After a few blocks, the high-end couture of the Gastown neighborhood gave way to something entirely different. Adele noticed slow-moving lumps of homeless people shuffling in alleyways. One man lay unconscious on a bus-stop bench with a hypodermic needle sticking out of his arm. Two bone-thin dogs crossed the street just in front of the taxi, their noses low to the ground searching for scraps to eat. The taxi driver cleared his throat.

"This is Downtown Eastside. Everything bad you find here. Police let it be - drugs, prostitution, and men like Yuri Popov."

The driver turned onto Hastings Street. The broken window structures looked like concrete corpses. Here the homeless no longer hid in the shadows. Instead, they congregated in large packs along the sidewalk. Some slept. Some spoke with others while Adele noted several appeared to be speaking only to themselves. One old woman stood with her scabbed arm stretched out in front of her and her mouth hanging open in a silent scream, pointing at the taxi as it drove by.

Maybe this wasn't such a good idea.

The driver chuckled. "See? This is no place for young woman like you. I take you back."

Adele shook her head. "No, please do as I asked. That's what I'm paying you for. Take me to a bar owned by Popov."

The taxi stopped in front of what appeared to be a burnt-out three-story brick building. "This is it."

"Here? Are you sure?"

The driver nodded. "Listen. You hear music, yes? Windows are blacked out so people can't see inside from street. You go little ways down alley. There will be big man at door. He'll let you in. They like it when young women come to see inside. They say it is good for business."

Adele could hear and feel the thump of a heavy bass beat.

"And this place is owned by Yuri Popov?"

The driver shrugged. "Sure. Popov or people like Popov, they'll know who he is in there. You pay me more, I wait for you out here. That good plan, yes?"

Adele handed the driver twice the amount that was owed him for the cab fare. "Yeah, that'll work."

The driver looked down at the money and nodded. "Ah, you are American!"

Adele closed the door and walked slowly down into the dimly-lit alley. A tall, long-haired, bearded man wearing a leather jacket brushed past her. The sweet-green stench of marijuana hovered around him.

"Sorry about that," he said after bumping Adele's shoulder. She followed him toward a metal door outside of which stood a barrel-chested older man in a tight t-shirt and blue jeans. Half his face was covered in a tattoo of a snake. The music was louder and the stench of marijuana much stronger.

At the end of the alley, a woman was giving a bent-backed old man a blow job. Adele gasped. The sound made the man watching the door laugh.

"What's the matter, darling? First time in the big city?"

The tall bearded man looked behind him at Adele and snickered. The doorman's laughter vanished.

"She with you?"

The bearded man shook his head. "No, never seen her before."

The doorman stepped toward Adele. Deep lines ran down along both sides of his mouth. His tongue flickered out from between his lips.

"Welcome to the Skin Patch. What's a tasty thing like you want with a place like this? Looking for work? If you are, I can help with that. I do you a favor, and then you do me. Just let me know."

Adele forced a tight smile. "Thanks. I'll keep that in mind."

The door was opened. Adele walked into a narrow hallway. The walls and floor were painted dark red. The bearded man in front of her sped up and then disappeared around the corner. The thump-thump-thump beat was so strong inside the building it hurt Adele's chest. The sound mixed with that of laughter, cursing, hoots, and hollers. The hallway led to a wide, low-ceiling space. On one side was a bar. On the other side was a row of booths. In the middle of the room was a short stage with a single pole where a group of women, some younger, some older, danced naked. They took turns grabbing the pole and swinging around it with blank faces and eyes that looked out at nothing. A crowd of men sat in chairs around the stage, leering and laughing as they held up colorful Canadian two-dollar-bills with the stern-faced image of Queen Elizabeth on them.

Several men turned around to note and admire Adele's arrival. She moved toward one of the unoccupied booths to her left, sat down, and sent a text.

I'm here at a place called the Skin Patch. Won't wait long. You promised if I made it here you would meet with me. Come soon.

The message was to a recently retired Vancouver B.C. reporter Adele had started researching last year. His name was Denver Wakefield. He had been responsible for some of the most aggressive coverage of Vancouver's multiple crime syndicates during what was possibly the city's deadliest stretch of murders in the 1990's when wars broke out between rival gangs over a diminishing drug trade.

Wakefield was nominated for a Pulitzer Prize for his coverage, an award he publicly remarked he cared nothing for. "I just want the son-of-a-bitches responsible for all the blood in our streets to be put behind bars," he famously said. Adele was fascinated by his hard-charging methods and seeming fearlessness when bringing to light some of the darkest acts of his home city's most dangerous organizations. Last night before going to sleep she had messaged him explaining who she was and asked if he would be willing to answer some questions regarding Yuri Popov. Within an hour he responded that if she could make it to Vancouver the following day and find a place owned by Yuri Popov he would meet with her there. Adele was hopeful that meeting was about to take place.

"You here alone, honey?"

Adele looked up and found a thin, blue-eyed blonde staring down at her. The woman was dressed in a dark leather corset and matching mini-skirt.

"Alone or not, it doesn't matter – the minimum is one drink order an hour," she explained.

"Can I just get an ice water?"

The woman shrugged. "Sure - that'll be ten dollars."

"What? Ten dollars for water?"

"It's either that or you leave. Don't blame me. I'm just the help."

Adele slapped two U.S. five-dollar bills on the table which the woman snatched up with the speed of a striking cobra. "Be right back with your water," she said.

Women cruised the room asking men if they wanted a private dance. Most of the men said no. A few said yes. One man whispered something to a woman who wore nothing more than bright pink knee-high socks. She smiled. He stood up and followed her to the back of the other side of the stage where they both disappeared behind a black curtain.

Adele found it all depressing. She didn't consider herself a prude or inexperienced in the ways of city life. As a teenager, she had walked with friends late at night around Seattle's Pioneer Square district where drugs and violence were common. Bellingham, where she went to college, had areas every bit as edgy as its big-city cousins.

This was different, though. It was a far more grotesque level of depravity. The dancers reminded Adele of balloons that had been deflated of all happiness and self-worth. The men who devoured those women with their soulless eyes were less than human.

The water arrived ten minutes later, and so did Denver Wakefield. Hard-edged cheekbones jutted out from a thin face. His dark eyes darted around the room before finally settling on Adele. He ran a slightly trembling hand through his long and limp gray hair. His voice was dry leaves over pavement.

"Given you're the only fully-dressed woman sitting alone, I take it you're also the one who messaged me about Yuri Popov?"

Adele nodded and offered to shake Wakefield's hand. "Yes, I'm Adele Plank. It's an honor to meet you, Mr. Wakefield."

Wakefield didn't shake. Instead, he folded his arms across his chest and tilted his head toward the stage. The padded shoulders of his sports jacket were torn and frayed.

"How did you end up here, Ms. Plank?"

Adele recounted how she had called up various taxi companies until she came to where the dispatcher was Russian and how that led to a Russian driver bringing her to the Skin Patch. Wakefield lifted a brow.

"Well done. You passed your test. Few things are more valuable to getting to a story like this than the use of the natives. Taxi drivers are particularly valuable resources. Their jobs allow them to see and hear a great deal. I haven't been here myself in a decade, and that was after a man was stabbed in the chest right over there in front of the stage. Apparently, he said the wrong thing to one of the bouncers. He survived the attack, though.

The bouncer who stabbed him wasn't so lucky. Authorities found his body washed up on Wreck Beach three days later. I have no doubt Yuri Popov ordered the killing. You see, we are sitting in one of the safest places in the city right now. The last thing a business like this wants is attention from the authorities, so when an employee does something to bring about that kind of attention, that is an employee whose expiration date has run out. Consider that your first lesson on Yuri Popov. He was a killer."

Adele noted the use of past tense. "Was?"

"Yes, he's more like me these days: long in the tooth and put out to pasture. You know, I could really use a drink."

It took Adele a moment before she realized Wakefield was asking her to pay for it. "Oh, of course!" She motioned to the woman who had brought the water. When she arrived at the booth, Wakefield gave her a wolfish smile.

"A double-Scotch on ice please and if the gentleman pouring needs to skimp on one or the other I'm happy to do without the ice but not the Scotch. The Scotch is sacred! And please be swift. I'm parched."

The drink arrived much sooner than Adele's water had. Wakefield downed it in one gulp and immediately asked for another. He caught Adele watching him and sighed.

"I'm an admitted alcoholic, Ms. Plank. That's what three decades covering bastards like the ones who own a place like this will do to you. Keep that in mind as you happily set off wrapped up in your own idealism to save the world. You should know the world doesn't want to be saved. It took me some time to learn that, and it's been an especially hard lesson."

Wakefield's second drink arrived. This time he just sipped it. His hands were no longer trembling.

"I've followed your contributions to that little island newspaper of yours. Don't be flattered. I read everything and everyone. My own competitiveness demands it. I do appreciate your style, though. The human-experience-driven narrative you incorporate is comforting."

Adele thanked him and Wakefield wagged a finger.

"No, we're not here to stroke each other's egos. You have questions. I might have answers. I'm old. Time is no longer a luxury I get to enjoy, so let's get to it."

Adele locked eyes with Wakefield. "What do you know of Sergei Kozlov?"

Wakefield shrugged. "Besides the fact he's dead? Killed by your sheriff, right? Sergei was a runt by Vancouver standards. Without the link to Popov, he wouldn't have been respected much, if at all. Petty crimes. He was too soft to really rise up in the ranks of Popov's crew. I'm guessing that's why he was given the San Juan Islands assignment. Something went wrong, and Sergei was on the outs. I still have plenty of sources on the street who were sharing rumor-mill stuff about that. A name came up a few times. One you'll know."

Adele waited. Wakefield finished his drink and ordered a third. A dancer came by and asked him if he'd like to go back to a private room. He shook his head and gave her an apologetic smile.

"I'm afraid I'd only disappoint you."

The woman left. Wakefield told Adele the name.

"The name is Roland Soros. Popov was working something with Soros – something big. I assumed it was the Cattle Point project I read about in your paper. There was lots of chatter on the streets here about it. Apparently, Popov had made promises to people in Moscow. When the deal with Soros fell through, those promises were broken, and Moscow wasn't happy. That left Popov financially stretched thin and increasingly vulnerable. He's fighting to recover and that can't be easy for a man his age."

"So Popov is desperate?"

Wakefield nodded. "Yes, absolutely. He's losing his footing here in Vancouver. This isn't an entirely new development. It's been happening for some time but when the Soros deal collapsed Yuri's situation became even more precarious. If you're a Russian crime boss, the last thing you want is to make Moscow unhappy. You should also know that Popov's interest in the San Juan Islands isn't new. It goes back many years. The islands have been one of his financial cash cows for a very long time."

Adele had to mentally push the pounding music out of her mind to focus on Wakefield's words. "What do you mean?"

"You accepted a position with *The Island Gazette* a couple years ago, correct?"

Adele nodded. "That's right."

"Just prior to that there was a seismic shift in Popov's drug trade business. Washington State voters legalized marijuana. Yuri Popov is rumored to have overseen one of the most profitable marijuana import operations into Washington State for some thirty years. Authorities here in B.C. have personally told me it was upwards of ten-million-dollars annually and a majority of that was going right through the San Juan Islands. Popov was happy. Moscow was happy. And the previous San Juan Islands County Sheriffs who Popov was likely paying off month after month and year after year to maintain his access to the islands for delivery of the drugs, were happy. Yuri Popov was a force to be reckoned with.

"When marijuana was legalized in your state, it left Popov scrambling to replace the sudden economic shortfall in his operation. It's alleged he turned to prescription drug imports, but that is work-intensive, involves offshore factories, and even greater payoffs to drug company employees and multiple government agencies. The scenario is far more complicated which results in far less simple and lucrative profit potential.

"Please understand that what I'm telling you is speculative. I can't prove any of it. No one will go on record. That doesn't mean it isn't true. I'm certain it is. I know Yuri Popov well. I know his business, his contacts, and the people he has paid off to survive and avoid prosecution. This is the world we live in. The difference between a cop and a criminal is a matter of perspective. Our schools don't educate but indoctrinate. Healthcare doesn't treat illness it invents it in order to create the need for the drugs being sold to fight it. The media doesn't find information, it destroys it and invents something else to replace it. Everything is part of a pre-determined narrative and everyone and everything merely another brick in the wall of that narrative. Yuri Popov has survived and even prospered in that grim world, but I believe his time is running out. He put too many of his own eggs in the Roland Soros basket and is now overextended. He owes Moscow a great deal of money, and I don't believe Popov currently has the means to even begin paying it back. This strip club? It hasn't been owned by Popov for three years. He gave it over to a front group controlled by Moscow interests."

Wakefield brought the drink to his lips, threw his head back, slammed the glass on the table and then ordered another. "Regarding the Cattle Point entertainment complex you wrote about in your paper that Roland Soros was planning to build and that I suspect Yuri Popov was heavily invested in. When your Mr. Soros pulled the plug and donated all that land to the county for a drug treatment facility my goodness, how that must have enraged Popov! He's killed men for far-far less. I would advise Mr. Soros to keep himself well-protected. It's my understanding Popov isn't finished with the San Juan Islands. There's talk of a movie being filmed there, and that means there's money to be made. Apparently, that's the only thing keeping Moscow from putting a bullet into the back of his head. It's hardly a secret how fascinated Moscow is with Hollywood. Moscow, the Saudis, the Chinese, they're all pouring hundreds of millions into the studios hoping to someday make billions. My guess is Popov is using a potential film deal as leverage to keep himself alive for just a while longer."

Adele took out her phone and pulled up the surveillance camera footage Samantha had copied from the Sheriff's Office that showed the mysterious blonde woman with the Russian accent. Adele pushed play and handed the phone to Wakefield.

"Do you recognize this woman?"

Wakefield's mouth fell open. He looked up at Adele.

"Where was this footage taken?"

"Friday Harbor."

Wakefield replayed the video then put the phone down and pushed it back towards Adele. He looked around the club while leaning over the table.

"The woman in that video is a killer who only answers to Moscow. Her name is Liya Vasa. She's the daughter of Vlad Vasa, a Moscow crime lord and one of the most feared men in the world. If you have a member of the Vasa family poking around your islands, that's a *very* serious problem. Liya rarely works alone, though. She has a younger brother named Visili who is her attack dog. They're both killers, but he's the one who most often sticks the blade in deep. I mean that literally. Knives are Visili's thing. That's his weapon of choice. Men, women, children…it doesn't matter. He'll kill anyone. Have you seen him on the islands as well?"

"I wouldn't know. I don't have any idea what he looks like."

"Trust me. If you see him, you'll know. He's a big, brutish thing with a scar that runs down the entire left side of his face. Rumor has it Liya put it there during an argument they had when they were children."

"Murderous siblings including one with a face-length scar? Sounds like a Russian mafia cliché."

Wakefield lifted his glass like he was making a toast. "And like all good clichés this one is based on truth and the truth is Liya and Visili Vasa are to be avoided. My advice to you is to stay clear and pray your paths never cross."

"Is that what you did as a reporter? Avoid conflict with these kinds of people?"

Wakefield sighed and shook his head.

"No, I didn't and look where it's left me. I'm twice-divorced living alone in a closet-sized studio apartment just two blocks removed from this hell-hole of a strip club slowly but most certainly drinking myself to death. At least when I was working these criminals feared what I might report. Now I'm just a tired old thing with stories to tell that no-one wants to hear. The world has moved on and left me behind. I despise Yuri Popov and would like nothing more than to see him get what he has deserved for so long but at the same time, I understand his frustration and his fear. We were men once. We are men no more. I pity him almost as much as I pity myself."

"I don't have time for pity Mr. Wakefield. I'm trying to protect my home and the people I care about."

"Please, Mr. Wakefield was my father. Call me Denver. That's what my friends call me – what few I have left. Is there anything else I might help you with?"

Adele nodded. "Yes. There's a former Washington State patrolman named Dan Walser who is handling the inquiry into the Sergei Kozlov shooting. Have you heard of him?"

Denver stared up at the ceiling with narrowed eyes. "The name sounds familiar. I tell you what, I'll look into it. I have years and years of notes going back decades. The kind of stuff you can't find on the Internet. I'll review my materials and see if I come across this Walser. I do know Yuri was bribing law enforcement on both sides of the border when his marijuana import business was booming. It's possible Walser was one of those on Yuri's payroll."

Adele stood up and again extended her hand. This time Denver shook it as he gave her a warm and grateful smile.

"I wish you luck, Ms. Plank. Please be careful. If I find out anything on Walser, I'll be in touch."

Adele thanked Denver for his help and returned outside where she found her taxi still waiting. The driver appeared relieved to see her again. Adele wondered if it was because she was OK or if it meant he was certain to earn more cab fare, not that it mattered. She had been away from the islands for less than a day but was already anxious to return.

Once back on the Chris Craft Adele wrapped herself up in a sleeping bag and tried to get some sleep. She planned to leave for the islands at first light. She lay on her back staring up at the stars and thought of Roland. Where could he be? Was he OK? Would he ever return home?

Adele imagined Roland on his sailboat with that sly smile on his face looking up at the very same stars she was. She felt a little tug on her heart, a sense of something having been lost. She feared she might never see him again.

Chapter 15

"Where'd you go?"

Suze was driving Adele back to Friday Harbor to pick up her MINI.

"Just looking into something."

Suze gave a half-grin. "That kind of answer means you don't want to talk about it. Say no more. By the way, I spoke with Bess this morning. She seems to be hanging in there. She isn't sure about any memorial plans, just yet. Oh, and there's some good news! She told me that Walser returned the printing software to her. Jose should already have it back online by now. Looks like you'll be good to go for the next issue."

Adele's phone rang. It was Lucas.

"Have you heard about the special council meeting tonight?"

"No," Adele replied.

Lucas sighed. "Yeah, they wanted to do it behind closed doors - an executive session. I told them if they're going to ask for my resignation they do it in public."

Adele switched the phone to her other ear. "What? They want you to resign? Why?"

"Apparently Walser has concluded the inquiry. Samantha gave me a heads up that it doesn't sound good. When I got the call from Councilman Box about the special meeting, his tone suggested the council wants me out. I'm almost positive that's what they'll be voting on tonight."

"Lucas, this doesn't make any sense. You didn't do anything wrong. Sergei had a gun. You had no way of knowing it wasn't loaded."

"Councilman Box mentioned the bad media coverage has the council concerned given the troubles the department had a few years ago with the high-profile Decklan and Calista Stone situation. He said they're worried it could hurt tourism. I was brought in to clean up the department after that mess, not create *more* scandal. That's how Box put it to me, anyway."

"I don't give a damn what Councilman Box thinks. What poor media coverage is he talking about? That Marianne Rocha? She's a joke - a big city reporter with an anti-police agenda. Don't give up on this Lucas. I'm here with Suze now. I'll let her know what's going on. We'll get the word out about the meeting tonight. If the council is attempting to push you out, there will be a whole lot of voters there telling them to back off."

Lucas didn't sound convinced. "I appreciate the effort, Adele. This feels like a done deal, though. I'm not saying it's right. Clearly, I'm being railroaded, but if a majority of the council wants me out, then I don't think there's much I can do about it. They're the ones who appointed me. If I had been voted in, it would be different. I'd have the votes of the people to justify my staying regardless of what the council wanted."

"Then that's what you'll do Lucas. Whether the council supports you or not tonight, don't you dare end your campaign for sheriff. You keep running, and you'll win. I know it."

"After tonight, I wouldn't be so sure, but I appreciate the vote of confidence. We'll just have to see how all this shakes shout. By the way, have you heard anything from Roland?"

Adele suspected Lucas's question was more than casual. "No. Do you think we should be worried?"

"Not yet. After our earlier conversation about where he might have gone, I looked into it. Seems he bought himself a sailboat recently. I'm guessing you already knew that, though. Maybe he's just out somewhere playing with his new toy. Still…"

"Still *what*, Lucas? Spit it out."

"I don't know. It just seems weird – the timing of it all. Roland disappears, Sergei basically uses me to commit suicide, and Walser suddenly shows up for what seems to be the sole purpose of getting me removed as sheriff. It would be nice to have Roland's version of what he thinks might be going on is all I'm saying. My gut tells me he might know more than the rest of us put together do. He's been tight with the council for quite some time. I remember him telling me once they were the best council money could buy."

"No, that isn't *all* you're saying, and you know it. When it comes to you and Roland, there's always more going on than just what's being said. Especially when you're the one doing the talking."

Lucas went silent. Adele knew she had hurt his feelings. She quickly changed the subject away from Roland.

"I'll be at the council meeting tonight. Don't lose faith in how much this community cares about you."

"I haven't lost faith, Adele. I'm just a realist. The council is going to move against me. I can feel it. I'll see you tonight."

Adele put down her phone. She could feel Suze's eyes on her.

"Did I hear you right? The council is going to force Sheriff Pine to resign?"

Adele nodded while staring out the passenger window. "Lucas sure seems to think so. There's a special council meeting tonight. He thinks they're going to vote against him."

"Well, that's just insane. It's like you said – self-defense, right? How in the world could that lead anyone to want to push the sheriff out? I know some of us worried the council might have lost its way, but I didn't actually think they would go after Sheriff Pine. None of this makes any sense."

Adele couldn't argue with that. Suze was right. Normally what was happening to Lucas wouldn't seem possible. Things weren't normal, though. Not since Sergei's death and Dan Walser's arrival.

Suze promised to spread the word about the special council meeting. She dropped Adele off at her car and drove off. Adele stood next to the MINI under the summer sun contemplating her options. Two blocks away she could see the top of the Soros family bank – Roland's bank.

Roland disappears. Lucas might lose his job. Walser attacks the newspaper after threatening me that I could go to jail for my support of Lucas. It's like we're being picked off one by one - all of us who had anything to do with shutting down the Cattle Point project.

Adele recalled the name of the woman running the bank in Roland's absence – Sandra Penny. She hopped into the MINI and sped off. She hadn't yet met Sandra. Adele decided it was time she did.

It was the first time Adele had been inside Roland's bank. The entrance was a clear glass door that opened up into a small lobby with a leather couch and matching chair. The floor was dark hardwood. The décor reminded Adele of Roland – stylish without being pretentious. A young female teller stood behind a counter on Adele's right. To her left was a door with a sign that indicated a conference room.

"Hello, can I help you?" the teller asked. Adele walked to the counter. The rubber soles of her shoes squeaked against the tile floors.

"Is Sandra Penny available?"

The teller, whose tag indicated her name was Emily Styles, flashed a friendly smile. "Do you have an appointment?"

Adele started to say no when Emily's brows shot up. "Oh! You're the newspaper writer – Adele Plank. You're good friends with Mr. Soros."

Adele nodded. "That's right."

"Wait one moment while I ring Ms. Penny's office upstairs."

Adele waited. She could hear the bank building's air conditioning unit humming outside.

"She said to go on up Ms. Plank. I'll show you the way."

Adele followed Emily to the back of the bank where a staircase ran up along the wall. "It's the first office on the right. She's expecting you. Can I get you something to drink?"

"No. I'm fine. Thank you."

The stairs led to a narrow hallway with just two doors. The first was on her right just as Emily said and the other was at the end of the hall. Adele knocked on the first door.

A woman's voice answered. "Come in."

It was a small office. Sandra Penny stood up from behind a modern glass and steel frame desk. Adele was surprised by how attractive she was. Long blonde hair tumbled over narrow shoulders and framed a full-lipped, strong-jawed, thirty-something face that reminded Adele of a Vogue model. Sandra reached across her desk to shake Adele's hand.

"It's nice to finally meet you, Adele. Mr. Soros has mentioned you more than a few times around here. Please, have a seat and tell me what I can do for you."

Adele sat down. She decided to put aside small talk and get right to it.

"Have you heard from Roland since he left?"

Sandra's tone instantly went from friendly greeting to all business. "No."

"Do you know how to reach him?"

"No."

Adele didn't buy it. "Really? What if there's an emergency here at the bank? He didn't leave you any contact information?"

Sandra crossed her legs, picked off a bit of lint from her skirt and then stared at Adele for a moment before giving an answer. "When Mr. Soros left he indicated he wasn't sure when he would be back. I assure you he left the bank's business in capable hands – *mine.* Everything here is fine. When Mr. Soros returns, it will be as if he had never left. He hasn't had a vacation in a very long time. Frankly, I was happy to see him getting away for a while."

"Have you known Roland long?"

Adele hadn't thought to ask that question. At first, she wasn't sure why she did. When Sandra smiled, Adele knew. She was jealous.

"Yes, I've known the Soros family since I was a girl. I knew Mr. Soros's grandfather. He hired me as a teller when I was just out of high school. The Soros family gave me a chance to work hard and work my way up. Now I'm the bank vice-president. I remember Mr. Soros coming in here when he was very young. I never imagined then I would be working for him now."

"You don't look much older than Roland."

Sandra revealed her model-perfect smile again. "Why, thank you! That makes me feel good. I'll grudgingly admit I celebrated my forty-third birthday six weeks ago."

Adele didn't want to like Sandra, but she couldn't help it. She felt guilty about her initial feelings of jealousy.

"Have you been visited by a man named Dan Walser?"

Sandra nodded. "The gentleman overseeing the investigation into the shooting? Yes, he came in a few days ago with the same question you just had regarding Mr. Soros's whereabouts. And before you ask, I gave him the same answer as the one I gave you; I don't know."

"What about Randall Eaton?"

Sandra frowned. "I don't recognize the name. Who is he?"

"He's an FDIC investigator. Are you *sure* he hasn't been here?"

"This is a bank, Ms. Plank. I'm certain I'd notice if someone from the FDIC showed up. Why would this Randall Eaton be coming here? I've received no notification of any compliance issues. We remain a bank in good standing."

Adele decided to drop the subject. She didn't want to have to explain how it was Lucas who had told her about Randall Eaton's investigation into Roland's banking activities.

"Well, if he does contact you, I'd appreciate you letting me know. And the same goes for if you hear from Roland. Some people are starting to get a little worried.

"I'll let you know if Mr. Soros *wants* me to let you know, Ms. Plank. Otherwise, you won't hear from me. I am very loyal to the Soros family, and I intend to continue being so. Unlike you, my business isn't other people's business."

Adele wasn't bothered by the slight. I came with the territory of being a reporter.

"I'm not here for a story, Ms. Penny. I'm here as Roland's friend."

Sandra stood up and straightened her jacket. "Will that be all?"

Adele said yes. Sandra offered to walk her back down to the lobby. When they reached the exit, Adele noticed a row of black and white pictures hanging on the wall behind the couch. Sandra pointed to them.

"Those are of the Soros family – Mr. Soros's grandparents. The one on the far right is Mr. Soros with his grandfather."

Adele put her face up to the photo. Roland stood just a little more than knee-high in front of his grandfather. Next to them was a middle-aged, stern-faced nun. Roland's smiling grandfather was handing the nun what appeared to be a check.

"Where was this taken?"

Sandra smiled. "Mr. Soros told me that was in front of the monastery on Shaw Island after his grandfather's…"

Sandra's words trailed off. Adele waited for her to continue. When she didn't Adele prodded her to do so.

"After his grandfather's *what*?"

Sandra lowered her voice. "Mr. Soros once told me his grandfather had a nervous breakdown. He despised hospitals, psychiatry, medications and so chose to have the nuns take care of him for a while. Mr. Soros said his grandfather remained behind the walls of the monastery for more than a month helping them to grow food, repairing the structures, cleaning, whatever they asked of him he did. That's a picture of him donating a check for fifty-thousand-dollars as a sign of his gratitude for their help in nursing him back to health. It was a great deal of money back then. The family has never been ashamed of that episode. In fact, it's just the opposite. They have kept that photograph on the wall as a reminder that they are no better than their customers. Their family has had struggles and adversity just like everyone else's."

Adele found it hard to look away from the photo. Roland looked so small and vulnerable holding onto his grandfather's pant leg while staring up wide-eyed at the nun.

"It looks like the nun might have scared Roland a little."

Sandra smiled. "Oh yes, Sister Mary Ophelia – not a woman to be trifled with. I was told once that even the Native Americans around here admire her. She's something of a legend to them. They call her the fixer of broken things. It's said creatures great and small come to her to be made whole again."

"She's still alive?"

Sandra nodded. "I believe so. I haven't heard otherwise."

Adele thanked Sandra for meeting with her. Sandra promised she would let Adele know if she heard anything from Roland or if Randall Eaton showed up asking questions. The air outside was much warmer outside. During the council meeting tonight Adele knew the temperatures were likely to get downright hot.

Chapter 16

Lucas stood alone in the dark outside the entrance to the county council meeting room. He looked up at Adele and then dropped his head. Adele could tell something was wrong. There were no lights on inside the building. She stopped. The two dozen or so people who were walking just behind her on their way to the council meeting stopped as well.

"Sheriff Pine, what's going on? I thought there was a meeting?"

Lucas straightened to his full height and nodded. "Yeah, there was. The council held an executive session already. It wrapped up twenty minutes ago. They already voted. I can't tell you who voted what because it was a behind-closed-doors session. The county could sue me if I disclosed that information to you. What I *can* say is that they put me on indefinite suspension pending negotiations for termination of services. It's done. I appreciate everyone showing up tonight on my behalf but it's over. The council members have already gone home. As of this moment, I'm officially no longer your sheriff."

Angry murmurs erupted behind Adele. She moved closer to Lucas.

"This can't be it, Lucas. You can still fight it. You *must* fight it."

A male voice cried out from behind Adele. "That's right! We won't let them get away with it. I say we pay the council members a visit to their homes. Tell them to their face what we think of them. You had every right to shoot that scumbag dead. I'd have done the same!"

Lucas held up his hands in front of him. "No, please, there'll be none of that. For now, I just want some time to process all of this. It's best everyone just go back home. Again, I appreciate all the support. I really do. I'm tired. I'm sure most of you are, too. We'll still see each other. This is still my home. What happened tonight won't ever change that."

A line formed in front of Lucas. One by one the people who had come to speak to the council on his behalf shook his hand and thanked him for his work as their sheriff. Some offered hugs. A few shed tears. Tilda Ashland was one of the last to stand in front of Lucas. She looked into his eyes, tilted her chin upward and gave him a tight-lipped smile.

"You are and have always been an honorable man, Lucas Pine. What happened tonight was an injustice, and this community will not allow it to stand. You have friends, important and influential friends. Our voices *will* be heard. I promise you that, and I am not a woman who goes back on her word. Until then, not for a single moment are you to allow those three pathetic politicians to define who you are. Do you understand?"

Lucas nodded. "Yes, ma'am."

Tilda nodded back. "Good. Now I'll leave you with Adele. I'm sure she has a lot to say. I suggest you listen. Of all the friends I mentioned that you have this little one here might be the toughest and most capable of all."

Lucas glanced at Adele and chuckled. "Yeah, I think you're probably right about that Ms. Ashland."

Tilda left Adele and Lucas alone. An army of moths swarmed under the glow of a nearby street lamp. Lucas let out a long sigh.

"As much as I saw it coming I'm still in shock. It doesn't seem real. Every member of that council has known me since I was a kid. They knew my parents. Two of them were my father's patients – the same two who voted against me! What the hell happened, Adele? How'd this all go so sideways so fast?"

"I don't know, Lucas. I'm working on figuring it out."

Lucas jammed his thumbs into the front pockets of his jeans and smirked. "Let me guess. I have to wait until the next issue of the paper to read about what you've been up to?"

Adele smiled. She was relieved to see Lucas handling the loss of his job so well.

"That's right. You have to wait just like everyone else."

Adele's tone became more serious. "I found out some things about Yuri Popov and am hoping to be able to prove a definite link between him and Walser. Stay tuned."

"Once you start chasing a story you don't give up, do you?"

Adele liked hearing the admiration in Lucas's voice. "I guess so. I just hope I can find out what's really going on in time for you to get your job back. Speaking of which, you're not going to stop your campaign are you? You're still running for sheriff, right?"

Lucas nodded. "Absolutely. I'd love to shove an election win right back in the council's face. That may not be the noblest reason for a campaign, but I'd be lying if I denied that's how I feel."

"Did you say two out of the three on the council voted against you tonight?"

"Uh-huh."

"Can you tell me who those two were?"

"I'm not supposed to. You couldn't use it in the newspaper. They'd know I was the one who told you."

Adele looked around to make sure they were still alone. "This is off the record."

"I tell you what. I'll clue you in on some of what happened during the executive session if you do something for me."

Adele waited to hear what Lucas wanted.

Lucas smiled. "Go fishing with me tomorrow morning."

"What?"

"Yeah – fishing. There are just a few days of lingcod season left. I say we head out first thing in the morning and see if we can't hook into a monster ling. Word is you picked up a new boat. Around here you're not a true captain until you get a bit of fish blood on the deck. We go out early. After that, you'll have the rest of the day to work. If we do catch something, you can swing by my place later for dinner. I promise the taste of a fresh-caught ling will blow you away. You'll want to go right back out to try and get another one."

"With everything going on you really want to go fishing?"

Lucas shrugged. "Sure, why not? I've wanted to get some fishing in all month. I can count on one hand the number of ling seasons I've missed my entire life. Besides, it's not like I have a job to get to right now. Might as well take advantage of all this free time. Meet you at your slip in Roche around seven?"

Though she wasn't looking forward to having to get up so early, Adele was happy to finally have an opportunity to catch a ling. Among the locals, the fish was prized above all others with only the king salmon giving it a run for most-loved catch-of-the-day status. She agreed. Lucas smiled.

"Awesome. I know just the spot where we might hook up. I used to go out there with Roland when we were kids. We spent way more time on boats than bikes. Between the two of us, we'd pull a half-dozen monster lings out of there every year."

The mention of Roland's name was like a silent wall that suddenly dropped down between them. Lucas's smile faded. Adele looked away then cleared her throat.

"Have you heard anything yet about where he might have gone?"

Lucas shook his head. "No – nothing. I wouldn't worry, though. Roland can take care of himself."

A car approached the area where Adele and Lucas stood. She had never seen it before, but that wasn't unusual given it was tourist season when hundreds of new vehicles drove off the ferries every day. The car slowed down then sped away. It was too dark for Adele to make out who was driving.

"I spoke with Sandra Penny earlier."

Lucas glanced at Adele. He seemed eager to hear news about Roland. That made Adele wonder if he was actually more worried about what might have happened to Roland than he was letting on.

"Did she have any information regarding Roland's whereabouts?"

"No, but she told me something else I found interesting. Randall Eaton hasn't been to the bank to meet with her. She had no idea who he was."

"Really? That doesn't make any sense."

"Did you do any kind of background check on Eaton?" Adele asked.

"I couldn't. I was on leave during the investigation. I didn't have that kind of access. I suppose I could ask Gunther or Chancee to run a check on him. You think Eaton might not really be who he says he is?"

"I think at this point anything is possible. I certainly wouldn't take his introduction to you at face value. He sure isn't acting like an FDIC investigator. How do you investigate a bank you've never even been to?"

Lucas nodded. "OK, I'll call in a favor to Chancee. She'll have a peek at him for us. I'll let you know what she finds out. Until then are we still on for fishing tomorrow morning?"

Adele said yes. She offered to give Lucas a ride to his home, but he declined, saying a long walk would do him some good. After a quick hug, he left. Adele walked to her MINI. She was about to open the driver door when she heard another vehicle coming toward her. She turned around and saw it was the same car that had driven by once already and just like before it slowed down.

Adele made a mental note of the color and style.

Dark blue four-door sedan. Windows appear to have a dark tint.

When Adele tried to read the license plate the car's motor roared and its tires chirped as it drove off. She caught a glimpse of a large man behind the wheel. She couldn't be certain, but it looked like he was glaring at her. Then the car and its driver disappeared into the night.

On her way back to Roche Harbor Adele glanced into her rearview mirror several times certain she'd see the same car following her. She didn't. Soon she was safely back in her sailboat with the companionway door locked and the porthole window curtains drawn. With Lucas coming by in the morning to go fishing Adele went to bed early. She didn't fall asleep right away, though. Her mind was too busy creating possible scenarios about who was really behind the council's move to remove Lucas as sheriff. She knew Yuri Popov was likely using Walser as his pawn, but it was shocking how quickly Walser was then able to manipulate the council to go along with whatever Yuri was planning.

Sleep didn't stop Adele's mind from trying to piece together a frustratingly difficult puzzle as one dreaming sequence drifted into another until finally, her subconscious settled upon something Denver Wakefield had said when discussing Yuri Popov and his connections to the notorious Vasa family – namely Liya Vasa's murderous sibling Visili.

She has a younger brother named Visili who is her attack dog. They're both killers, but he's the one who most often sticks the blade in deep. I mean that literally. Knives are Visili's thing. That's his weapon of choice. Men, women, children…it doesn't matter. He'll kill anyone… If you see him, you'll know. He's a big, brutish thing with a scar that runs down the entire left side of his face. Rumor has it Liya put it there during an argument they had when they were children.

Adele's eyes shot open. She sat up so fast she bumped up against the sleeping quarter's low ceiling. She cried out, rubbed her head and then focused on trying to recall the brief glimpse of the man behind the wheel of the car that had twice driven by her in Friday Harbor.

He was a big man with a scar that ran down his face. I'm almost certain.

After that, Adele didn't fall back asleep.

She waited for morning.

Chapter 17

All Lucas brought with him was a thermos, two fishing poles, a tackle box, a gaff hook, and a smile.

"Great boat."

Adele grinned. "Thanks."

Lucas looked over at Adele. "You OK?"

"Yeah, I'm just tired - didn't sleep much." Adele had decided not to tell Lucas about her possibly seeing Visili Vasa in Friday Harbor. Doing so would lead her to tell him about the trip to Vancouver which would then force her to have to listen to him lecture her about being more careful.

"I'm sorry. Hey, if you need some rest we don't need to go out today. It can wait."

Adele steered the Chris Craft around a buoy. "No, I want to go. You said ling season is almost over. The morning air will wake me up. Just give me a few minutes. Besides, we could both use a little downtime from all the crap we've been dealing with."

Lucas poured a cup of coffee from the old dented green metal thermos he had earlier told Adele had belonged to his father. He handed the cup to her. She took a sip and nodded.

"It's good. Thank you. So, where are we headed?"

Lucas pointed at the GPS navigation screen above the steering wheel. "We're going to hit that area just north of Waldren Island – Boundary Pass. See that smaller green spec on your GPS? That's Skipjack Island. We'll work the bottom between those two points. It doesn't get fished nearly as hard for ling as some of the more well-known spots like north Sucia and Spencer Spit down around Lopez Island. As long as the current isn't ripping too hard and we can get our bait close to the bottom we should be able to hook up."

"These fish are really worth it, huh?"

Lucas folded his hands behind his head as he leaned back in the Lancer's passenger seat. "You'll be begging for more. You'll see."

Adele idled out of Roche Harbor into the two-foot chop of Spieden Channel. It was going to be a bumpy ride to the fishing hole. The Chris Craft took it in stride. The bumps that were felt were never jarring, courtesy of the heavy hull and its deep-water design all which helped to keep them from spilling their coffee.

"Man, this thing really does ride smooth. You picked this up from Gentry, huh?"

Adele nodded. "That's right. He put a lot of love into her."

"He sure did. And Gentry knows his stuff. You did well."

The chop continued until they reached the backside of Sucia where the waters suddenly turned glassy-green smooth. This allowed Adele to accelerate to a much faster speed. Lucas gave her a thumbs up and an ear-to-ear grin. He shouted over the din of the motor.

"Yes indeed, this thing has some get up and go!"

The high cliffs of Spieden were a starboard-side blur as the Lancer sped north toward Waldron Island. The bow thumped into a few large swells, causing a spray of mist to cover the windshield. Adele turned on the wipers, took another sip of coffee, and confidently kept going.

Soon they came upon the large tree-speckled rock that was Ripple Island where Brixton Bannister had lived in self-imposed seclusion for so many years. Adele made a mental note to check in with Brixton once she returned to Roche Harbor. She worried Vincent's rejection of him might have pushed Brixton's already fragile pride and ego into some kind of crisis.

"Hey! Check it out!"

Adele's eyes followed to where Lucas was pointing. It was a pair of playful Dall's porpoises crisscrossing in front of the Lancer's bow. With their shiny dark backs and white bellies, they looked like miniature Orca whales. The water hissed and bubbled behind their small dorsal fins. Adele checked the GPS and noted the Chris Craft was doing twenty-five knots. She marveled at how swiftly the six-foot-long sea mammals could cut through the water. The porpoises continued swimming in front of the boat for another quarter mile before suddenly diving deep and disappearing.

Once they entered Boundary Pass, the waters turned rough again. Adele reduced the speed and glanced at the GPS. The western shoreline of the three-thousand-acre Waldron Island was on their right. The island was home to just a hundred or so residents. It was without utilities, public docks, ferry service, and proudly continued a "go away and leave us alone" reputation that residents of the other islands traditionally respected.

"Waldron attracts an interesting collection of personalities, I'll tell you that. In all the years I've lived here, I've only ever set foot on it once. It was a public disturbance call that came in via shortwave radio. Someone's cat tore up a neighbor's dog."

Adele gave Lucas an "I don't believe you" look. He chuckled.

"I kid you not. That was the complaint. I make the trip by boat out to Waldren and am met at the dock by two women. One of them has this dog on a leash, and its snout is all scratched up. An ear is torn. It's missing a clump of fur on its shoulder. It was part German Sheppard or something - pretty big dog. I'm thinking there's no way a cat would tangle with it. Well, the woman with the dog insists that's exactly what happened. She was a fierce older lady. Thin but strong like a wire. And she's really ticked off. The other gal was even older and a touch on the frail side. She isn't saying much so I start to think maybe her cat really did mess up that poor dog which of course makes me have to go check out what kind of cat could do that. At that point,

I'm seriously intrigued. I mean that has to be one tough cat, right?

"The owner of the cat tells me to get on the back of her moped. Her place is deep near the center of the island about a mile away. There are hardly any motorized vehicles on Waldron. The roads are more a maze of paths that disappear into the trees that connect one end of the island to the other. I'm about three months into my job as sheriff, this big bad former military guy and football player sitting on a moped driven by a seventy-something old lady and I'm holding on for dear life. She's really gunning it. We're leaning into corners, whipping by trees that are no more than a few feet on either side of us and I think I'll never live it down if I end up dead on the back of that moped.

"We reach her home. It's not much more than a hand-built lean-to with a door on it in the middle of a clearing surrounded by these huge fir trees. We get off the moped, and she warns me to walk behind her and not make any sudden moves. She says Mr. Whiskers is still in a bad mood on account of his fight with the dog. I really felt like I had just walked into some version of the Twilight Zone.

"Then, the old lady smiles and starts clapping her hands. 'There he is!' she says. I look up and see the biggest damn cat I've ever seen in my life running toward us. It was huge, like something that should have been hunting the Serengeti!"

Adele put her hand over her mouth to try and stifle a giggle. Lucas wagged a finger at her.

"I'm not kidding. The cat was a monster! It bounds up to the old lady and then makes a full stop and starts to check me out. I'm a tall guy, right? I swear the cat's head came up to my knees. It had to have been thirty pounds easy. The old lady says to give him all the time he needs to check me out. The cat is making this growling noise while it sniffs my pant legs and shoes and starts to rub up against me. The lady smiles and tells me I'm now Mr. Whiskers-approved."

Adele tilted her head back and laughed. "I never knew you were Mr. Whiskers-approved!"

Lucas rolled his eyes. "Yeah, it was a real Clint Eastwood moment for me on Waldren Island. I advised the cat owner that she might want to contribute to the injured dog's vet bill. She refused, saying the dog had come into her yard when Mr. Whiskers was on patrol. That's the term she used – *on patrol.* When I presented this information to the owner of the dog, she admitted the dog had been wandering when the altercation occurred and that was that. I gave both women a warning to keep their animals away from each other and made the trip back to Friday Harbor. And that's my Waldren Island story. Not too bad, huh?"

Adele looked at Lucas. They shared a smile.

Adele looked away. "Not bad at all, Lucas. Now I know what I'll get you for Christmas this year."

"What's that?"

Adele bit down on her lip and grinned. "A cat calendar."

Skipjack Island was straight ahead. It resembled a three-clawed hump with trees growing out of its top. Adele slowed down and pulled up the fish finder screen on the GPS. It detailed the rough and rocky sea floor below. Lucas pointed at the screen. His eyes were wide and bright.

"See those little ravines that cut across the bottom? That's where you find the lings waiting for their next meal. Put it in neutral, and we'll see what kind of drift we're working with."

Lucas moved to the back of the boat and opened his tackle box. He put two large chrome-colored jigs at the end of both lines then glanced down at the water. Adele was fascinated by how quickly and delicately his large fingers tied the knots in the line.

"It looks to be nearly a two-knot drift. Going to have to be careful not to snag. These ten-ounce jigs should still be heavy enough to get us to the bottom, though. You have any good fishing tunes?"

"What do you want to hear?" Adele asked.

"How about some *Simple Man* by Skynyrd? That usually works for attracting the bigger fish."

Adele pulled up *Simple Man* on her phone and plugged it into the boat's stereo. When the music started Lucas's boyish grin returned.

"Yeah, that's the good stuff right there."

He handed Adele a pole and gently turned it over in her hands. "Click that little lever down but keep your thumb on the line. Otherwise, you might get a bad tangle."

The heavy metal jig disappeared into the dark water. Lucas looked back at the fish finder.

"We're at seventy feet. It should be just a few more seconds until you feel a bump. That means you've hit bottom. When that happens, move the lever on the reel back into the locked position, so no more line goes out. Then turn it over and quickly reel up about ten feet of line, so the jig is just off the bottom. That'll help to make sure you don't snag it on a rock."

Adele felt the bump Lucas described. She locked the reel, turned over the pole, and reeled in some line. Lucas nodded.

"Well done. Raise the tip of the pole up about four feet then let it fall back down and repeat over and over again until Mr. Ling decides to have a bite. That's called jigging."

"How will I know when I have a bite?"

"Trust me. You'll know. A big ling doesn't mess around."

Lucas took a position on the other side of the boat and let his own line out and then started jigging as well while Lynyrd Skynyrd sang of troubles that would come and troubles that would pass. The song was nearly over when Adele's arms were suddenly pulled downward. She cried out and tried to pull the pole back up, but it wouldn't budge.

"Crap, I think I'm stuck on the bottom."

Adele felt another strong tug and worried the pole might be ripped from her hands. Lucas started to reel in his line.

"That isn't bottom. That's a fish! Hold on."

Lucas put his pole away and stood next to Adele. When the line started to pull out, he calmly told her to let the fish take it.

"It's a big one. The more it works, the more tired it'll get. Too often people make the mistake of trying to force a ling to the boat before it's worn out. You can get away with that with the smaller ones but not with a big boy like this."

"Do you want to take over? I don't want to screw up and lose it."

Lucas shook his head. "If you lose it, that's fishing Adele. It's just like life. There are no guarantees. That's what makes it so exciting and often frustrating. There's a chance you could spend the next ten minutes fighting this thing, and it could get away. You're not going to do that, though. I can already tell. You're a natural."

Adele grunted as she tried to pull the tip of the pole up. Her forearms started to ache.

"I'm not sure I share your confidence in me but thanks for the compliment."

Lucas put his hand on Adele's shoulder. "You're doing great. Just keep at it."

Adele was able to reel in a few feet of line, and then a few feet more before the pole dropped down so far the tip nearly went into the water. Lucas whistled.

"That's a strong fish. We're going to eat well tonight."

Adele gritted her teeth and lifted the pole up and then reeled some more. She kept repeating this process until she spied the first glimpse of color from the ling. It was a speckled gold-brown – and big.

Lucas grabbed the gaff hook. "Keep reeling slowly. Bring it to the side of the boat. You're doing great."

Adele's face was hit by saltwater flung at her by the ling as it thrashed on the water's surface. She pulled up on the pole and then nearly fell backward when the line snapped. "Oh no!" she cried.

Lucas lunged so fast Adele thought he was going to fall overboard. The Chris Craft lurched to the side. The gaff hook plunged into the water. The ling thrashed some more. Lucas let out a triumphant shout as he lifted the big fish out of the water and brought it into the boat.

Adele's eyes went wide. "Look at that thing. It's so ugly!"

"So ugly it's beautiful," Lucas said. He yanked the hook out of a mouth that was the size of his fist. Adele flinched when he smashed the butt end of the gaff hook over the ling's head. Then he stuck the gaff into the fish's mouth and lifted it off the deck.

"I'd say it's close to forty pounds. Here, hold it up so I can get a picture. This is quite a catch for a first-timer!"

Adele grabbed onto the gaff. She had to use both hands to hold the fish up. She was impressed by its rows of sharp teeth, especially the two biggest ones in the upper center of its mouth that gave it the look of a buck-toothed aquatic vampire. The top of the ling's hard head was rust-colored cartilage that matched the color of its fins and tail. Its belly was soft and yellow.

Lucas took several pictures with his phone while Adele's arms trembled from the effort of holding the fish up in front of her. When she could finally put it down, she was again amazed by its size and other-worldly appearance.

"You sure about how good these things are supposed to taste?"

Lucas used a towel to wipe up some of the ling's blood from the deck. "How's the saying go? Don't judge a book by its cover? Well, that monster there is like that. You just stop by my place for dinner tonight, and you'll see. I promise."

With the ling wrapped in the towel and secured at the back of the boat, Adele sat down behind the wheel. She looked over at Lucas who was leaning over the side to wash his hands off in the sea water.

"You want to stay out here and try to catch one?"

Lucas straightened and shook his head. "The one you caught is plenty. No sense in being wasteful. It's a lot more than we'll be able to eat ourselves in one sitting. We'll have to freeze most of it. How about we just take it slow getting back and enjoy the water and this new boat of yours? And this time you get to pick the tunes."

That was fine by Adele. She put the Lancer in gear and accelerated up to a leisurely and comfortable eighteen knots. She felt Lucas's hand wrap around hers. He glanced at her and then his eyes darted away as if he had suddenly been struck by a temporary bout of shyness.

"Thank you, Adele. I needed this. It was the perfect start to the day."

Adele smiled and squeezed his hand. She turned up the stereo's volume, sat back in her seat, and enjoyed the sensation of the gentle up and down motion of the Chris Craft as it moved across the water.

Lou Reed's voice accompanied them home.

It's such a perfect day.
I'm glad I spent it with you.
Oh, such a perfect day.
You just keep me hanging on.

Adele heard Lucas singing. She looked over at him. His eyes were closed. For the first time in a very long time, he seemed completely happy. She began to sing along with him.

It really was a perfect day.

Chapter 18

Brixton Bannister looked like a very different man than the one Adele had first come to know as the Ripple Island hermit, and it wasn't a change she approved of. In fact, she took all of his attempts at an improved appearance as a sure sign he was falling down the slippery slope of increasingly desperate insecurity. His skin had an odd yellow-dark tint that betrayed his repeated use of a tanning bed. The hair was carefully groomed, the skin clean-shaved, and the eyebrows and fingernails meticulously manicured.

He had become a stranger in his own body, a far too-pretty reflection of the man he once was. Adele had first marveled at the initial transformation from mysterious island recluse to hopeful soon-to-be-again movie star, but now it was clear that transformation had gone too far.

Brixton's teeth were so white they defied the laws of nature. His smile faltered.

"What is it?"

Adele shifted in her chair. She was sitting with Brixton in the corner of the lobby inside the Roche Harbor hotel where they had met for afternoon tea.

"I was about to ask you the same thing. What's going on with you?"

Brixton shook his head. "I don't know what you mean."

"Yes, you do. Something is bothering you. My guess is that something involves Vincent Weber."

Brixton frowned. "There is that, yes. I went to see him yesterday. He's a mess. I'm certain he was drunk. It boggles the mind how someone so emotionally lost could create a screenplay as compelling as his. Frankly, I'm not even sure I want to be associated with the project anymore."

Adele heard the lie behind Brixton's words. Being in Vincent Weber's film had become an obsession marked by every extreme he now took to try and improve his appearance.

"He continues to say how he's worried my participation would be a distraction. How my look doesn't fit with his vision for the character of the writer. He thinks I'm too soft. He wants someone with more of an edge. It's the same crap he's been telling me for weeks, and no matter how hard I try to convince him otherwise there doesn't seem to be any changing his mind."

Adele sipped her tea. "How did you respond to him when he told you these things yesterday?"

Brixton sighed. "I reminded him of how I spent years living by myself on a rock surrounded by water. That if it's an edge to the role he wants I'm the actor to deliver it. Nobody could possibly understand the character of the writer more than me! Vincent sat there like he didn't even hear what I was saying. He went on to mention a new investor who had her own ideas about the film. He said she was prepared to put a significant amount of money into it so the film wouldn't be held back by the studio's budget restrictions. Then he ordered another drink and went on ignoring me altogether."

Adele locked eyes with Brixton. "Did he say the name of this new investor?"

Brixton shook his head. "No. All I know is that it's a woman who apparently has access to a lot of money. I swear, when Vincent was talking, I thought of using a knife to prove to him exactly how much edge I have. I'd like to take that edge and gut him with it."

Adele looked around the hotel lobby worried that someone might have overheard the threat. "Don't talk like that Brixton. You're not that person."

Brixton grunted. "Aren't I? I was in Hollywood a long time before I disappeared, Adele. I lived an entirely different kind of life then, full of things I wish I could forget. I can't, though. I remember – I remember *everything*."

"Then why are you trying so hard to get back to that old life? Why do you care about being in Vincent Weber's movie?"

"I want to be a part of something important. I've already been famous. I've already been a star. I don't want that. What I *do* want is to be an artist. Vincent Weber's screenplay would allow me that opportunity, but the drunken son-of-a-bitch is taking it from me."

"For someone who says they don't want to be a star you've sure made an effort to look like one. The whitened teeth, the fake tan, I wouldn't be at all surprised if you went in for a full-body wax job."

Brixton's eyes flared. He opened his mouth to say something but then looked down. Adele groaned.

"Geez, you really did get a wax job! Brixton, don't you understand all of this work on your appearance is probably a big part of Vincent Weber's unwillingness to let you be in his film? You *do* look too soft and pretty for the part. And there's something in your eyes too. It's desperation. Weakness. Those aren't the qualities you would want to bring to the role of Decklan Stone. Decklan is one of the most real, down-to-earth people I know. This old Hollywood version of you that you've fallen back into? It's nothing like Decklan. I'd go so far as to call it an insult to him."

Brixton sat silent and unmoving. He lightly gripped his teacup with the tips of his perfectly manicured fingers and then cleared his throat.

"Gee, I guess you should tell me how you *really* feel."

Adele leaned forward and waited for Brixton to look at her. When he finally did, she gave him a smile.

"I'm your friend. Sometimes friends have to be honest with each other. You've lost who you are to the person you used to be. I'm hoping you'll fight to get the real you back. That's the Brixton Bannister I want to know. As for Vincent Weber and his film, I have an idea about who this new investor he was telling you about is. She's not anyone you would want to be associated with. In fact, I think Vincent is getting in way over his head. Trust me. You don't want to get caught up in any of that."

"You know who the investor is? Vincent said it was foreign money. Is that true?"

Adele pushed up against the back of her chair. "Not just foreign money – *bad* money. Please listen to me when I tell you that you're better off staying away from Vincent Weber. There'll be other opportunities for you – and on *your* terms."

Brixton sighed. "Maybe you're right." He ran his fingers down both sides of his face. "Do I really look that ridiculous?"

Adele had made her point. She didn't see any reason to bruise Brixton's ego any further.

"You're a beautiful man, but that beauty has nothing to do with what's on the outside. You were most interesting to me when you smelled of saltwater and sweat. I'm not saying you don't clean up well, because you do. I just think you've lost your way a bit and it's time you start to find your way back. Besides, Decklan and Calista Stone aren't happy with Vincent Weber either. I think they might actually exercise their first refusal rights and stop the project altogether."

Brixton's eyes widened. "Really? What has them so upset?"

Adele shook her head. "I'm not comfortable speaking for them. I just wanted to let you know you're not the only one who has issues with Mr. Weber."

Brixton stood up. "You know what? I think you're right. I've let my love of Vincent's screenplay turn into an obsession. I don't need to do that. I'm Brixton Bannister. I was a top box office draw when Vincent Weber was still in diapers. He should be begging me, not the other way around."

Adele stood up as well. "That's right. You're the big name, not him."

Brixton straightened the sleeves of his sweatshirt, looked around the lobby, and nodded. "Yeah, that's just what I'm going to tell him when I withdraw my interest in the film. It was people like him who made me want to disappear from the industry in the first place. I'd forgotten how much I despised cockroaches like Weber. He isn't an artist. He's just another self-destructive bug. You take care, Adele. I'll see you again soon."

Brixton walked outside. Adele watched him go. She wasn't the only one.

"Whatever you said to him it appears to have put some bounce back into his step."

Adele turned around to find Tilda standing over her. "I just told him the truth."

Tilda pursed her lips. "Hmmm, truth can be a dangerous thing for some to hear. Do you believe Brixton actually took your words to heart or was he merely playing the part of the man you wish him to be? He *is* an actor."

Adele had already considered the possibility Brixton had just faked his appreciation for the advice she had given him. She hoped his reaction had been sincere. Then again, perhaps was even a good enough actor to fool her.

Chapter 19

Lucas didn't answer his phone. Adele was hoping to confirm what time he wanted her over for dinner to enjoy the ling cod she had caught that morning. She left a message, sent a text, waited several minutes, and then called again.

Still no answer.

It was almost eight. Lucas had told Adele to plan for dinner around seven but that he would call her first to remind her. That call never came, and now he wasn't responding to the multiple messages she had sent him over the last hour. She wasn't yet worried but knew it was unlike Lucas to not follow through and even more unlike him not to get back to someone. That is, unless something was wrong.

Adele pushed that thought out of her head and decided to just go to Friday Harbor to find out what was going on. On the way to the parking lot, she had to dart between the slow-moving throngs of tourists who clogged the Roche Harbor docks.

The drive there was uneventful. Adele parked in front of Lucas's home, walked up the steps of the front porch and pushed the doorbell. The blinds were drawn. She was reminded of the time last winter when she had found Lucas passed out in the bathtub upstairs after a night of heavy drinking following his father's death. Adele scampered down the steps and hurried to the back of the house.

The door to the kitchen hung open. Adele stepped inside and scanned the room. The ling sat in the sink, its body partially covered in ice. A fillet knife was on the counter. Pieces from a broken coffee cup were scattered across the floor. A chair was knocked over. The table had been pushed up against the wall with enough force it left a hole in the drywall.

All evidence pointed to a struggle. She stood frozen just inside the door trying to hear if anyone might still be in the house.

"Lucas? Are you here?"

Adele took another step into the kitchen. She thought she heard breathing coming from the living room.

"Lucas?"

Someone cleared their throat. Startled, Adele fell back and struck the open kitchen door with her shoulder.

"Come in. I have been waiting for you."

The voice belonged to Yuri Popov. Adele took out her phone to call 911.

"If you wish to see the sheriff alive again we must talk. They could return. Please come inside now."

Adele continued to hold her phone. "What did you do with Lucas? Where is he?"

Though she couldn't see him, Adele heard Yuri groan. "We have no time to waste. Sit down with me. I am an old man. I will not hurt you."

Adele walked into the living room and found Yuri sitting on the couch. There were no lights on. His face was partially hidden in early-evening shadow. Adele looked around to make sure they were the only ones there. Yuri motioned for her to sit down in the chair next to him. Adele remained standing.

"I'll ask you one more time. Where is Lucas?"

Yuri grimaced as he sat up. What thin strands of hair he had left on his head were greasy and disheveled. His voice was weaker, his eyes dull and bloodshot. He had helped himself to some of Lucas's whiskey and held a half-empty glass of it between his hands.

"They took him. That is all I know."

Adele felt a chill run through her. She already knew who "they" were.

"Liya and Visili Vasa – they're the ones who took Lucas?"

Yuri grunted. "You are a good reporter. Yes, they are the ones who grabbed your sheriff from this home almost two hours ago."

"But you don't know where they took him?"

"I don't *want* to know. They find me, they take me too!"

"What does Liya want with Lucas?"

Yuri grinned. "See? You already know Liya orders her brother Visili. You *are* a good reporter."

Adele was growing impatient. She sensed time was moving against them – especially Lucas.

"What do they want? Are they going to hurt him?"

Yuri emptied his glass in a single gulp. "You mean to ask if they will hurt him more than they already have. Yes, they will. And if they think he is no longer of use they *will* kill him. You must understand that. There will be no body found. No evidence. No sheriff. Nothing. It will be as if he had never been."

Adele took a slow, careful breath as she fought to stay both calm and clear-headed. "OK, you're obviously not here just to tell me your Russian friends took Lucas. What do you want?"

Yuri again pointed to a chair. "Sit."

Adele shook her head. "I'm not your dog and if you don't start telling me something I can use to save Lucas, I'm calling the police."

Yuri placed the glass on the coffee table and then calmly pointed a gun at Adele's face. "No, you will *not* call the police. If you do that your sheriff is dead and both you and I will likely be next. So sit - NOW."

Adele glared at Yuri as she sat down. "How do I know Liya and Visili aren't working for you? They could have taken Lucas on your orders."

"You have to trust me. I have no authority over Liya. I am Vancouver. She is Moscow. Now she is here on your islands and where Liya and her brother go blood *always* follows."

"That's your fault. You brought them here."

Yuri shrugged. "Perhaps, but was it not your friend Roland Soros who brought me here as well? He took my money for his Cattle Point project. Then he shuts the project down. There were people, *powerful* people involved in all of that. So does that not make Roland also responsible for Liya and Visili? I say yes. If you point the finger of blame at me, you must also point it at him."

Adele wouldn't admit it out loud, but Yuri was right. Roland was at least somewhat responsible for this mess.

"What does the Cattle Point project have to do with Liya and Visili taking Lucas?"

"It has *everything* to do with it. And you, yes *you*, are partly to blame for our troubles as well."

"Me? Why?"

Yuri put the gun down and held his empty glass up in front of him. "First I need a refill. There was no vodka, so this will have to do."

Adele thought of telling Yuri to go to hell and then leaving. Then she remembered Lucas was out there somewhere being held prisoner by two murderous Russian mafia siblings. If getting Yuri Popov another drink would help to get Lucas back then so be it. After returning from the kitchen and handing him the glass, Yuri took a drink, smiled, and then leaned back into the couch as if he didn't have a care in the world.

"That is better. Thank you. Now, where were we?"

"You're going to explain how I have anything to do with Liya and Visili coming to the islands and taking Lucas."

Yuri grinned. "Yes, that's right. Well, it is simple, really. You see, I have done much business through these islands for many-many years. During that time—"

Adele recalled the information Denver Wakefield had shared with her. She interrupted.

"During that time you oversaw a sizeable marijuana sales operation. You paid off local law enforcement and other officials to ensure the money kept flowing. It was your cash-cow, the foundation of your criminal enterprise. When Washington State voters legalized marijuana, you suddenly found yourself dealing with a greatly reduced revenue stream. You were stretched thin. You turned to illegal prescription drugs and started funneling them through the islands as well, but that was work-intensive with higher risk and less reward. You're old, set in your ways. You wanted something easier."

Yuri stared into Adele's eyes. His voice was a growly croak.

"Please continue."

"Somehow you found out about Roland's Cattle Point project. I'm guessing it was a member of the county council who tipped you off. It's likely the same one who has more recently been helping to push Lucas from his position as sheriff. You use Sergei as your point of contact between Roland and yourself. You offer funding. The kind of funding that can bypass normal bank underwriting requirements. You didn't have that kind of money available to you, though. Your business was in decline. So, you turned to your contacts in Moscow. You promised them big returns on their investment. They gave you the cash which you then used to loan to Roland.

"And then Roland pulled the project and donated the land to the county which effectively shut you out of any involvement with Roland for good. He did pay you back what he owed. Did you send that money back to Moscow? Or, did you use at least some of it to keep yourself afloat in Vancouver hoping to buy yourself some time? Either way, Moscow couldn't have been happy. That's why Liya and her brother are here. Which leads me to ask why I shouldn't just give you to them so they'll leave the rest of us alone?"

Yuri scowled. "I must admit you have done a very good job putting pieces of my puzzle together, but if you were to give me to Liya, you would be helping the ones who killed your friend. I don't think that is what you wish to do."

Adele stood up. "What do you mean? Lucas isn't…"

Yuri held up a hand. "No, no, no, not the sheriff. I am talking about the old newspaper man."

Adele sat back down as her mind pulled up the memory of Avery's explanation of what happened right before he fell down the stairs. It was one of the last things he had said before dying.

I was outside the office. There was a smell in the air like, uh, lavender. It was quite pronounced. I heard a noise behind me, and then…that's all I recall. I woke up here.

"You think Visili killed Avery?"

"Was the old man stabbed to death?"

Adele shook her head. "No. He fell down the stairs outside his office and then died later in the hospital of a heart attack."

Yuri nodded. "Yes, so if he was not stabbed, then it was not Visili. It was Liya who pushed the old man down. Perhaps she was merely trying to warn him to stop with the stories about me and organized crime. Those stories were making our business here far more difficult. Moscow was not happy with your little newspaper and the role it played in ending the Cattle Point project."

Adele's fingers dug into the chair. "Are you saying it's my fault Avery died?

Yuri shrugged. "I am saying there is plenty of blame to go around. I am not the cause of all of your troubles. You have done plenty to make your own."

"No. You don't get to do that to me. I might have reported on some of the things you were doing, but that doesn't change the fact you were the one doing them. How many lives on these islands have you made worse, Yuri? The drugs, the intimidation, the bribes, everything you touch you poison. But you couldn't buy Lucas, could you? And eventually, Roland cut you off as well. And now Moscow demands you pay a debt you can't afford. Look at you. You're all alone. No entourage. No goons to protect you. I say let Liya and Visili have you and be done with it."

Adele started to stand but was stopped when Yuri again pointed the gun at her. "Don't threaten me, stupid girl. I know you more than you think. I know you demand justice for the death of your friend. Liya will not stop with me. She can smell the money to be made here on the islands. Do you know who her father is?"

"Yeah, Vlad Vasa. He's a Moscow crime lord and apparently the worst of the worst. You're small-time compared to him."

Yuri's eyes blinked rapidly, a gesture that suggested to Adele he hadn't expected her to already know so much about his Moscow connections. He cleared his throat.

"That is correct. Vlad is as you say the worst of the worst. Liya and Visili are the arms and the hand, but Vlad is the mind and the body. You hand me over to them, and you are forever involved with him. That is how this all works. You are either an asset, or you are a liability which means you either work for him, or you are dead. Vlad Vasa is a very powerful man…but not a subtle one."

"Is Walser working for you or for them?"

Again Yuri's eyes went blink-blink-blink. He set the gun down, looked away, took a sip of whiskey, and then shrugged.

"Walser *was* mine. That is no longer true. He is Liya's toy now."

With a weapon no longer pointed at her Adele was able to relax just a little and focus on getting more information from Yuri.

"What's Walser's connection to Vincent Weber?"

This time Yuri didn't merely blink. He flinched. Then he tried to lie. It was a clumsy effort and didn't fool Adele for a second.

"Vincent Weber? I don't know the name."

"He's a director. I'm almost positive you at least know of him. Walser certainly does."

Yuri's jaw clenched. "Ah, the director. Of course! Perhaps I told Liya about the proposed film. Convinced her it would be a good investment. She is as naïve as she is arrogant about such things. It bought me time. It seems everyone in Moscow wants to be part of Hollywood these days. I know this. I used it. That is all."

"Who is the member of the council who was helping you to push Lucas out as sheriff so you could replace him with Walser?"

Yuri finished his whiskey, set the glass down on the coffee table and folded his arms across his fleshy chest. "Eh, that is not important. You and me, we have much work to do and very little time."

"What work is that?"

Yuri's eyes flickered with the light of a devious child. "We must give Vlad Vasa what he does not yet have. It is something he demands so that a proper example can be made. If you hope to see your friend the sheriff alive again, you must do this. There is no other way. There has to be a sacrifice of one to avoid a sacrifice of many."

Adele felt a tightening in her throat. "What are you talking about? What are we supposed to give Vlad Vasa?"

Yuri tilted his head upward. "It is not *what.* It is *who.* I told you. We give them what they don't yet have. We give them Roland Soros."

Chapter 20

Lucas was dead. The image Yuri demanded Adele see made that clear. Lucas was bound and gagged and hung naked from a rafter inside a warehouse like meat at a slaughterhouse. Fresh blood covered his chest and groin. Adele looked away, her stomach churning. She wanted to scream, to run, and to kill those who had murdered her friend.

"He suffered a great deal," Yuri chortled. "Look at his face. How his mouth hangs open like he is still screaming. You should not have delayed. I warned you this would happen if you failed to deliver Roland Soros to them. You did not listen, and now your sheriff is gone. If you continue to delay others will die as well. Perhaps the next one will be the hotel owner."

Yuri held his phone up in front of Adele. "I said look at his face. See the pain of his final moments and know you are the one responsible."

Lucas's eyes were open but vacant. Adele could see the gash across half his throat where Visili's knife had cut deep. Other similar wounds marked his chest, stomach, and upper thighs. Lucas had been forced to die slowly. Adele felt sick. She pushed Yuri's phone away and covered her mouth with a trembling hand. Sweat covered her face and stung her eyes. She stumbled backward.

"We need to get help. Call the authorities. I don't know where Roland is. We can't allow others to be hurt. Someone has to do something. Someone has to stop them. They killed Lucas. My god, they killed him!"

Yuri held a fat finger to his lips. "Ssshhh, there is no need for such noise. We cannot tell anyone about this situation. I already told you that if you do that more will die. Don't be stupid, girl. Be strong. Be smart. Listen to what I say."

Adele's phone started ringing. She reached into her pocket, but it wasn't there. The ringing became louder. Yuri's eyes narrowed.

"Who is calling you? It better not be the authorities. I warned you what would happen!"

Adele felt her chest tightening. She couldn't breathe. Tears ran down her face. The ringing continued. She looked around trying to find her phone. Yuri started to laugh.

"Stupid girl will get us all killed. Look at you crying. The brave reporter sobbing like a child!"

Yuri's face was close enough to Adele's she could feel and smell his hot, sour breath. His lips drew back into a snarl.

*"**You** killed him. You chose to protect Roland Soros, and now the sheriff is dead because of it. It's all your fault!"*

Adele felt the last of her humanity snap inside of her like a piece of thin twine stretched beyond its limits. With her fingers spread out like talons, she dug her nails into Yuri's face. Each thumb jammed into the soft center of his eye sockets. She ignored his screams. Even as he begged her to stop she pushed her thumbs in deeper until she felt the fleshy orbs of his eyes pop.

Yuri fell down. Adele jumped on top of him while screaming, laughing, and crying all at once. She straddled his chest, scratched and clawed at his face, tearing away strips of flesh, throwing them aside and then going back for more.

The ringing of her phone filled her ears. She still couldn't find it. The ringing wouldn't stop.

Adele opened her eyes and felt her heart pounding against her chest. The horrific images of the nightmare lingered.

Just a dream. A terrible, terrible dream.

Her phone lay on a table inside her sailboat. It continued to ring. She pushed herself out of bed and answered it. The number was blocked. Whoever was calling hung up. This was immediately followed by a text from the same mysterious number.

You've been on my mind girl since the flood.
Heaven help the fool who falls in love.

Adele had heard those words before. She did a quick Internet search and matched them to a song titled "Ophelia" by a band called The Lumineers. She pulled the song up on her phone and listened to it from beginning to end - twice. It was during the second listen that a tingle traveled from the top of her head to the bottom of her spine.

Adele knew who sent the message. More importantly, she knew where she would find him. It was nearly 5:00 a.m. The first hint of morning light would soon arrive. When it did, she would jump into the Chris Craft and be on her way.

Outside, the Roche Harbor air was cool and still. Nothing moved. Even the water appeared to still be asleep. The pinkish hue of brightening clear skies pushed back against the horizon's darkness.

Footsteps.

Adele turned around and looked up toward the marina entrance. She saw the murky outlines of two people standing just beyond the light of one of the resort's many antique lamp posts. Both were tall. One was slightly taller and broader in the shoulders. The shorter of the two stepped into the light. It was a blonde-haired woman. Adele froze.

Liya and Visili Vasa had come to Roche Harbor.

Adele was careful to keep herself in shadow as she crouched low and quietly eased herself behind the wheel of the Lancer. The sound of heavy footsteps drew closer. Adele untied the Chris Craft and pushed it out of its slip. It drifted backward until it was nearly forty feet from the dock. Adele watched and waited with her hand on the ignition, ready to make a quick escape.

"This is it," Visili grunted. He kicked the side of Adele's sailboat. After waiting for a response, he kicked it again.

"Are you sure?" Liya asked. Her voice was low and authoritative. The Russian accent made it even more so. Adele sat behind the Lancer's windshield holding her breath watching, listening, and waiting.

"Yes. Walser described it perfectly. This is where she lives."

"Perhaps she's staying in the hotel. Walser said she was friends with the owner, a woman named Tilda Ashland."

Adele inhaled sharply as she watched both Liya and Visili look back at Tilda's Roche Harbor Hotel. The last thing she wanted was to send the two Russian siblings Tilda's way. It was time to come out of the shadows. Adele turned the key.

The Chris Craft came to life. Liya and Visili's heads snapped back. Their eyes widened as they realized how close Adele still was to them. It was close enough Adele could clearly see the scar running down Visili's face.

"Get her - now!" Liya hissed.

Good luck with that, Adele thought. She pointed the bow toward open water and accelerated.

Adele heard Visili running down the dock. She watched him leap into an open-bow runabout. The boat wasn't his. He clearly didn't care. Adele stared at him. Visili stared back as he turned the boat's outboard motor on. He didn't untie the ropes that held the runabout to the dock but instead cut them with a long knife and then used that same knife to point at Adele. Visili's face broke out into a predatory grin. Adele was stunned by how quickly he had given chase. For such a large man he was incredibly fast.

She accelerated while heading toward the sunrise in the east. The water conditions remained unusually flat, the kind of water that allowed for speed. Adele glanced behind her. Visili was catching up. She pushed the throttle down even more. The runabout was much lighter than the Lancer which meant in such calm conditions it would also be faster.

Despite knowing that, Adele remained calm. These were her islands, not Visili's. She was determined to make that knowledge an even greater advantage than mere speed. Adele hugged the shoreline while heading toward Limestone Point on the northeast edge of San Juan Island. She considered going into shallower water but knew the Chris Craft would likely go aground long before the smaller runabout would.

A quick check of the illuminated GPS showed Neil Island and Rocky Bay directly ahead. Adele zipped toward the bay and then turned hard to port so that she would pass near the southern tip of Neil Island. She looked behind her hoping to see Visili having to slow down as he approached the Lancer's wake. The runabout didn't hesitate. It hit the wake at full speed sending water spraying several feet into the air. The bow lifted and then the entire boat came crashing back down. Adele's ears strained to detect any sign Visili had reduced his speed. She glanced behind her again and saw the runabout no more than a hundred yards away.

The Chris Craft glided across the water at nearly forty miles an hour. The diesel engine roared, sounding as if it didn't like being pushed so hard. The small little humps that broke the water's surface known as the Wasp Islands were a half-mile ahead. Beyond them loomed Adele's destination – Shaw Island.

The Wasp Islands were actually a collection of interconnected reefs that were notorious for destroying the running gear and hulls of boats and ships captained by men and women with limited knowledge of the area. Locals often referred to them as the "rock pile." Adele intended to drive right through them. The depth sounder chirped a warning that the bottom was suddenly no more than six feet deep. Adele's face was a mask of determined focus. She reduced her speed just slightly as she darted between the large rocks called Low Island and Nob Island. The GPS indicated the depth was now just four feet. Adele knew that if she were to hit something at such a high rate of speed, there would be no saving herself. It would be the equivalent of driving a car into a wall at forty miles an hour but without the benefit of a seat belt, airbags, crumple zones, or even brakes.

The last remnants of night had been almost entirely overtaken by the new day. Adele could clearly see the path in front of her. Visili was no more than fifty yards away.

The Lancer entered Wasp Passage, a mile-long waterway that separated Orcas Island and the smaller Shaw Island. The sunrise sent shimmering red and gold shards dancing off the glass-like water. Adele cursed the lack of waves. Just a little bit of chop would have made the going far more difficult for the smaller boat. Visili followed closer and closer. He was going to catch her.

Adele felt something hot cut the air inches from her cheek and then noticed the hole in the windshield. She turned around and confirmed that knives weren't the only weapons Visili used. He was pointing a gun at her. She saw the tip of it flash as he shot at her for a second time. She steered the boat from side to side hoping to make herself a more difficult target even as she knew that the closer Visili came to the Chris Craft the more likely the next bullet would find its mark.

The horn blast of the day's first ferry echoed across the water. Wasp Passage was one of the busiest ferry routes to and from the islands. Adele had never before been so happy to hear the sound. She pushed the throttle all the way down, crouched low, and sped toward the approaching ferry.

Visili followed. Adele crouched low behind the windshield. She wanted Visili to remain confident. It was her hope that confidence might soon be his undoing.

The ferry's horn wailed a warning at the two much smaller vessels that were crossing directly in front of its path. Adele had already tested the Chris Craft once before by using a ferry's wake. What she intended to do this time was weaponize that wake and use it against Visili. He might have had the slightly faster boat, but she was confident it was also a far less seaworthy one.

Adele sped down the side of the ferry toward its stern. She was so close to the massive three-story vessel it felt as if she could reach out and touch it. She heard the low-pitched thrum of its 8000 horsepower diesel engine that vibrated the water all around her.

Once she reached the rear of the ferry, Adele made a hard turn without slowing and during what few seconds remained before the collision, recalled Gentry describing how stoutly built the Lancer was.

"...rest assured there's almost an inch of hand-laid fiberglass below the waterline - real tough stuff. She'll take a pounding out there and shrug it off like it's nothing. Biggest twenty-three-footer you'll ever own. They don't make boats like this anymore. Cost too much. It's all thin sprayed fiberglass garbage. This here is old-school American made, just like me."

That claim was about to be put to an even tougher test than before. Visili was by then nearly parallel with Adele. He raised his gun and prepared to fire. Adele could see the lust for violence in his eyes and prayed the water would hit before the bullet did.

The tip of the Chris Craft's bow struck the wake. Adele was thrown forward. She let out a loud grunt and lost her breath as her chest pushed against the steering wheel. She gritted her teeth and looked to the side and watched as the front half of Visili's runabout disappeared under the water. She heard him cry out as the impact nearly tore the thin plastic windshield from the boat.

The Lancer launched upward and was temporarily air-born before crashing back down into the water. Adele was flung to side but managed to keep one hand on the steering wheel which she then used to pull herself back up into the driver seat – something Visili was unable to do.

While the Chris Craft continued moving forward Visili's runabout had come to a full stop. Its open bow had swamped.

The weight of the sea filling its hull pushed it further and further below the water's surface.

Adele let out a triumphant shout. Her plan had worked. Gentry had been right. The Lancer proved a far tougher vessel than most. It remained dry and running while Visili's boat had stalled as it took on more and more water.

Visili glared at Adele from across the widening stretch of sea that separated them. He stood in a sinking boat but if he was afraid he didn't show it. Just before turning past Shaw Island's Broken Point on her way to the island's marina Adele took one last look behind her. Hardly any of Visili's stolen boat remained visible. It appeared as if the water was swallowing it whole. Visili lifted his knife and pointing it at her. It wasn't the knife that made Adele go cold, though. It was Visili's madman grin as he calmly observed her escape.

Despite the rising frigid waters that surrounded him he was making it very clear he intended to see Adele again. Then the Lancer turned the corner, and Visili was gone.

For now.

Chapter 21

Adele had been walking for nearly an hour when she spotted an old woman sitting on a large flat rock on the side of the narrow gravel road that led from the secluded Shaw Island marina deep into the island's heavily wooded interior. The woman wore torn and tattered blue jeans that were tucked into the tops of her knee-high rubber boots and a heavy wool sweater with the sleeves rolled up to her elbows. Her long gray hair was braided and ran down her back behind her shoulders.

"Hi," Adele said with a quick smile. The old woman regarded Adele with unusual intensity. Her deep blue eyes narrowed.

"Hello, Adele. We've been expecting you."

Adele stopped. The woman pushed herself off the rock and stood up. She was small, lean, with a bent back that made her appear even shorter than she actually was. The lines that ran from the corners of her eyes and down the sides of her face deepened as she smiled.

"No need to be concerned. Everyone is welcome and safe here."

Adele frowned. "I'm not concerned. I'm confused. How do you know who I am?"

The woman shrugged. "I never said I know who you are. That kind of knowing takes time. I just said your name. Here, let me introduce myself. That way you won't feel you're at such a disadvantage because you'll know my name, too."

Adele looked down at the badly bent, arthritic hand that extended toward her, paused, and then briefly shook it. The woman smiled. Her deep-set eyes twinkled as she took her other hand and placed it over Adele's and squeezed it with surprising strength.

"My name is Mother Mary Ophelia. You can just call me Ophelia, though. Welcome to my home."

"How did you know I was coming today?" Adele asked.

Ophelia smiled again. "Our mutual friend told me you would be. He said he sent you a clue and that he was certain you would figure it out far sooner than most. And he was right. Here you are. Come, you must be hungry after your journey."

Despite her age, Ophelia moved quickly. Adele had to jog to catch up.

"I need to see him right away. It's an emergency."

"Yes, yes, as I just said, he's expecting you. We can discuss your concerns during our meal together. Until then let's walk and talk. It's another ten minutes or so to the monastery."

Adele walked alongside Ophelia and listened as she pointed out various examples of island plant life, gave an abbreviated version of the monastery's history which included details on how she came to arrive there when she was no older than Adele, and how great of a blessing she felt it was to have been able to live out her days on the island among its beauty and equally beautiful people.

The road narrowed further until it was little more than a dirt and grass path. Adele noted how the walk didn't seem to tire the old nun. They arrived at a gate built from aged wood planks. Beyond that gate was a fenced field of many acres. Adele saw cows, sheep, and goats eating away at the tall grass. When Ophelia pulled the gate open nearly all of the animals began making their way toward her. An excited baby goat bleated loudly and started to run.

Ophelia clapped her hands together, crouched low and then took the little goat into her arms. The goat nuzzled its nose against the nun's neck. Ophelia laughed, set it down, straightened her sweater, and motioned for Adele to follow.

"The main hall and sleeping quarters are this way. To your right is a hen house built during the Second World War. On top of that hill to the left are the stables. We only keep the animals in there during the coldest part of winter. The rest of the time they're allowed to roam free. The entire property is more than three hundred acres – plenty of room for everyone. Some call it strange. Others have described it as idyllic. Me? I just think of it as home – the only one I care to know."

"I saw your picture on a wall inside Roland's bank. You knew his grandfather."

Ophelia stopped and turned around. "That's right. Mr. Soros was very much like Roland - remarkably similar, in fact."

"How so?" Adele asked.

Ophelia took a deep breath. "Well, Mr. Soros was terribly ambitious. He was a good man but deeply flawed. He struggled with doing right or choosing wrong to his last breath. We all wage similar battles within ourselves of course, but for Mr. Soros, it was a war of greater extremes than most. We became good friends. And yet there were times, too many times perhaps, when he offered me nothing more than disappointment. It was not an easy friendship but instead a consistently complicated one. At the end of the day, though, I had no regrets. He was a beautiful man, complications and all. The monastery had a long period of financial difficulty years ago. If not for Mr. Soros's patronage it likely would not have survived. I will be forever grateful to him for that...and for so much more."

As Adele wondered if Ophelia's memories of Roland's grandfather went beyond mere friendship, Ophelia walked over to a pair of light brown cows and playfully scratched behind their ears. When she started to return to where Adele stood the cows followed her.

"This is Old Momma and her daughter, Flower. They're Jersey Cows, wonderfully gentle and loving creatures. I helped deliver Flower three summers ago. Old Momma is the best milk cow we've ever had here at the monastery and Flower isn't far behind. Between the two of them, they provide us with more than enough milk, cream, butter, and cheese. What we don't use we donate to local families in need. That's the real beauty of this place. It's truly self-sufficient."

The cow named Flower nudged Adele's thigh. "Give her a quick scratch, and you'll have a friend for life," Ophelia said.

Adele scratched Flower behind her ear. The cow's eyes partially closed as it let out a soft groan. Ophelia chuckled.

"See? She's just like her mother. These cows love to be scratched! I figure that's a fair trade for all the milk they provide."

Ophelia was on the move again. She pointed to a long, single-story building that sat atop a gently-sloped hill.

"That's the main hall. We gather there for prayer, reflection, and our meals. The cabins where we sleep are in the back."

A gravel walk path surrounded the building's perimeter and led to a ten-foot-tall, solid wood entrance door that was rounded at the top. Ophelia grasped the aged copper handle attached to the door, gritted her teeth and with a loud grunt, pulled it open.

"This door was heavy when I was a young woman. I'm certain it gets a bit heavier with each passing year. Three inches thick and cut from an old-growth tree that had been uprooted during a terrible storm that pummeled the area back in 1963. The wind cut across the Strait of Juan de Fuca and slapped our islands like God's hand itself! It was truly biblical. The sisters and I found the fallen tree, and with the help of a local woodsman it was cut and sold for lumber, but we kept just enough to craft what was then a much-needed new door. I was about your age when I helped to carve it out and put it here where it has hung ever since. All the sisters who were with me then are gone. I'm the only one from that time who still remains."

Ophelia knocked on the door. "That's the sound of memory. I take some comfort in knowing that when my time comes, a little something of me will remain here with this door so that I might continue to welcome friends and visitors to this place."

Adele found it to be a strange and beautiful thought. She reached out and ran her fingers over the door's rough, cracked surface.

"It really is quite a door."

Ophelia smiled and nodded. "As it should be. This really is quite a place! Come on in."

Adele stepped inside. Ophelia closed the door behind her. One of the few pieces of furniture Adele spotted was a long wood dining table that looked to have been made from the same tree as the front door. The floor was wood as well and was deeply scuffed and marked by countless footsteps over many decades. In the center of the room hanging from the ceiling was a single chandelier that gave off just enough light to keep the shadows confined to the corners of the room. Ophelia pointed up at it.

"That was a gift from Father John O'Toole of Seattle. He brought it here following the renovation of St. James Cathedral in the 1970's. He once stayed an entire summer here just a few years before his death in the 1980's. He always remarked how the islands were such a blessed place. He was one of my favorite guests and a bit of a rebel within the Church – brilliant and *very* opinionated. That's his picture over there."

Adele moved to the wall behind the dining table and looked up at a framed color photograph of a white-haired old man dressed entirely in black who appeared to be scowling at the camera. A much younger version of Ophelia stood next to him smiling. Adele's gaze then moved to another nearby picture. It was the same one that hung inside of the Soros family bank.

"Is that the photo you were telling me about?" Ophelia asked.

Adele nodded. "Yes, that's the one. You don't look very happy in it."

Ophelia shrugged. "I wasn't. Mr. Soros insisted on giving the monastery that check. It was fifty-thousand dollars - an outrageous amount of money. I felt guilty taking it from him. He could be very persuasive, though. I suppose that was a big part of his success."

Adele didn't think it was just the money that had made Ophelia appear so upset those many years ago. The check represented how Roland's grandfather had recovered from whatever emotional ordeal that led to his seeking recovery among the nuns of Shaw Island. That meant he was leaving the monastery which was what Adele suspected had been the primary cause of Ophelia's stern-faced appearance in the picture.

Adele watched as Ophelia's eyes lingered on the photo a moment or two longer before she turned and walked toward a hallway on the opposite side of the room. "He's waiting for you, Adele. Right this way. He's been staying in our guest cabin. You two can talk privately, and then we can all meet back here for some lunch. All the other nuns are at a conference in Seattle for the rest of the week, so it'll just be us. That's fine by me. I enjoy the quiet."

Ophelia opened a door that led to the back area behind the main building. The grounds were meticulously maintained with rows and rows of multi-colored roses, a sprawling herb garden, a large greenhouse, and a collection of circular Yurt cabins that dotted the landscape.

"It's the one at the very back with the grape vines growing on the side. Just follow the path and knock on the door. He was out mending a fence earlier this morning, but he should be back by now."

Adele walked toward the cabin. The gravel path crunched loudly beneath her shoes. She wiped the palms of her hands against her pant legs and wondered why she felt so nervous.

The cabin door opened. Roland stepped out wearing dirt-encrusted jeans and a sweatshirt. His normally combed hair stood up at various angles, unwashed and unkempt. The beginnings of a light-brown beard covered his face. He was holding a cat which he carefully set down by his feet before standing back up, crossing his arms and then leaning against the inside of the door frame. When he smiled, Adele tried not to smile back. She wanted to be angry at him. She was supposed to be angry. Roland was at the very least indirectly responsible for much of the troubles that plagued the islands, including the arrival of Liya and Visili Vasa and their taking Lucas hostage.

Roland cocked his head as he kept smiling.

Adele couldn't help herself.

She smiled back.

Chapter 22

Roland enthusiastically explained to Adele how the cabin he was staying in was the very same one used by his grandfather during his time at the monastery decades earlier. It had been hand-built by nuns in the 1950's and only had room for a narrow bed and one chair. Roland sat in the chair and offered Adele the bed. He pointed at the cabin's one window and told her how he had come to look forward to ending each day lying in bed while watching the sun disappear behind the tall trees outside. Adele listened politely. She was happy to see Roland but had many unanswered questions, and her concern for Lucas hovered over everything.

"OK, it's clear something is wrong. I thought it was just the clue I texted you, but I can see there's another reason you showed up here today. What's going on?" Roland asked.

Adele's fingers dug into the tops of her knees. She stared down at her shoes, took a deep breath and then looked up. She was trying very hard not to be angry. It wasn't easy. Roland's brows lifted as he waited to hear what she had to say. Adele detailed her troubles with Dan Walser and Yuri Popov, the bogus investigation Walser waged against Lucas, and Avery's sudden death. She then explained who Liya and Visili Vasa were, their interest in the film about Decklan and Calista that was to be directed by Vincent Weber, how they had taken Lucas hostage, and that Yuri was convinced that if she wanted to see Lucas alive again, she had to give them Roland. She finished by telling him how she had left Visili in a sinking boat on her way to the monastery.

"My god, I had no idea, Adele. If I had known…"

Roland went quiet. His head dropped. Adele waited for him to look up at her. After several seconds passed, he finally did.

"What? What could you have done Roland? Yuri made it clear the money he lost when you terminated the Cattle Point project was actually money that cost his contacts in Moscow. These people are killers. If it wasn't Lucas who was taken it would have been you and I'd be sitting here trying to find a way to get you back instead of him. Either way, this would be a mess and either way I'd be involved in trying to clean it up."

Roland shook his head. "No, you don't understand. These people, they're *my* problem. That's why I pretended to leave and came here to hide out. I was warned Yuri was getting desperate, that he was having trouble in Vancouver and might come to the islands to try and force me to help him out. I didn't want him involving you or anyone else. I figured if he couldn't find me he'd lose interest and go away."

Roland's explanation presented Adele with multiple questions, all of which made her anger toward him worsen.

"Who warned you about Yuri? Was it Randall Eaton, the FDIC investigator?"

Roland cocked his head. Normally he smiled when he did that. He wasn't smiling this time.

"You know about Eaton?"

"Yes. Lucas told me about him. I'm starting to doubt he's with the FDIC, though. I met with Sandra Penny at your bank. She said she'd never seen him. In fact, besides Lucas, it seems nobody has actually met him. So, who is he?"

Roland rubbed his forehead. Adele knew he was thinking about how he should answer. She didn't want to give him that time.

"I said, who is he? Stop trying to figure out a response. For once just tell me the truth – all of it."

Roland's eyes flashed annoyance. "I *did* have the FDIC looking into my business shortly after I moved all of my assets around so I could pay off what I owed Yuri following my donation of the Cattle Point property to the county. It didn't concern me too much, though. I was confident I had my regulatory bases covered with them. Then Eaton shows up one day at my house, flashes his FBI badge, and proceeds to explain how he's been working an investigation with Canadian authorities and Interpol on Yuri Popov for the last few years. He tells me about surveillance recordings between Yuri and Yuri's Moscow contacts regarding what should be done about their San Juan Islands problem. Eaton suggests I hide out for a while until they can close in on Yuri for good. He indicated it was to be a few weeks or a couple months at most. I refused at first. That's when he told me that if I stayed, the ones I care about could be caught up in the crossfire. That was the last thing I wanted, so I followed his advice. I left. I wasn't supposed to tell anyone, but I couldn't leave without telling you."

Adele scowled. "You used me, Roland. You were playing games. Sending me that text with the music link? Under different circumstances it would have been charming – but not now. Not with Lucas in so much danger. And what about that picture of you and your grandfather at the bank? Did you have Sandra make sure I saw it? She certainly seemed ready with her explanation of the photo's history."

Roland opened his mouth to respond then closed it tighter than it was before. The gesture confirmed Adele's suspicions. Roland had found time to make the threat of Yuri Popov a game. It seemed no matter how serious the events were that swirled around him, Roland always remained determined to make light of it. He straightened in the chair.

"I'll fix this. I'll get Lucas back. You'll see."

"Even before you left Lucas was already involved because of the Sergei shooting. Your leaving made things worse, not better. And where is Randall Eaton? If he's actually FBI why isn't he doing something? Why did he introduce himself to Lucas as working for the FDIC?"

Roland shook his head. "I don't know why he would have done that. Unless…"

"Unless what?" Adele asked.

"Unless he didn't trust Lucas. Maybe Yuri Popov isn't the only one Eaton is investigating. Perhaps he's investigating all of us – me, Lucas, you, the county council, anyone he thinks could have been benefiting from Yuri's operation."

As much as Adele found that scenario hard to believe she had to admit it was possible. It could also explain why Eaton had been keeping such a low profile since his earlier brief visit with Lucas. Eaton was likely still out there somewhere watching and waiting.

Roland leaned forward and put his hands over Adele's. "None of that matters right now, though. We need to help Lucas. If you want to blame me for all of this later, that's fine. I understand. But right now we need to work together. That's really why you're here."

Adele stood up. "Yeah, you're right. So let's go."

Roland stood up as well. "Go where?"

Adele hadn't thought that far ahead. "I guess we reach out to Yuri. Hopefully, he's learned by now where Liya and Visili are keeping Lucas."

Roland moved in front of Adele. "Wait, before we do that I think we should talk to Ophelia. She knows things."

"What things?"

"She knows a lot of history about the area and its people."

"Does Ophelia know about Yuri Popov?"

Roland nodded. "Yeah, she does - quite a bit actually."

Adele thought to ask Roland how an old nun would know about a Russian crime boss but then decided to wait and hear it from Ophelia herself. She followed Roland outside and walked beside him toward the monastery's main building. "You like it here don't you?"

Roland slowed. He looked out at the animals grazing in the field.

"I do. I understand why my grandfather came here and why he continued to support this place long after he left."

Ophelia had cheese, crackers, and wine laid out for them. She sat at the head of the table and motioned for Adele and Roland to join her. "It's a light meal and just a bit of wine. We'll eat first and then we can talk."

Adele hadn't realized how hungry she was until she devoured her first two mouthfuls of crackers and cheese. She finished her plate soon after and sipped from the half-glass of red wine, savoring its dark berry flavor.

"Roland, I assume you'll be leaving the monastery today?"

Roland swallowed the last of his meal and nodded. "That's right. I don't have a choice. I have to go back. A friend is in danger because of me."

Ophelia set her glass on the table and folded her hands in front of her. "I see. Would you mind telling me the nature of this danger?"

Adele glanced at Roland. He nodded. She cleared her throat and then proceeded to repeat to Ophelia the summary of events she had earlier shared with Roland. When Adele finished Ophelia thanked her.

"I know of Yuri Popov. He's been a cancer eating away at these islands for a very long time."

"How do you know…" Roland's question hung in the air unfinished. He sat back in his chair. Adele suspected he already knew the answer. Ophelia nodded.

"Yes, your grandfather had an arrangement with Yuri that was far longer and more involved than your own more recent one. It wasn't so much financial, at least not for your grandfather, as it was related to his trying to protect our quality of life here. Yuri was allowed to use the islands to shuttle his marijuana from Vancouver to the American mainland. In return, Yuri promised to keep the more dangerous drugs away from the islands. The lesser criminals feared his power. Your grandfather arranged to have local law enforcement look the other way where Yuri was concerned. As far as I know, no money was ever exchanged between Yuri and him. It was simply a matter of your grandfather accepting what he saw as a lesser evil to avoid the possibility of a greater one. He would allow marijuana to come through the islands in order to keep out drugs like cocaine and heroin. It certainly blurred the lines between right and wrong, but it worked. We never had a serious drug problem on the islands until the more recent deaths attributed to prescription drugs, deaths that I know Adele reported on in her newspaper."

"And then voters legalized marijuana leaving Yuri without a major revenue stream," Adele added.

Ophelia nodded. "That's right. And as the events you just described to me prove, he's become increasingly desperate. Roland, your grandfather, made a deal with the devil. That devil outlived him and so left you as a target for Yuri due to their earlier relationship. The sins of your grandfather have been passed on to you. Today an even greater devil has taken Yuri's place – a two-headed one named Liya and Visili. Evil, *true evil*, has come to our islands. What your grandfather worked so hard to keep away is now here."

Ophelia suddenly held up her hand as her eyes narrowed. She looked toward the door.

"Someone is coming."

Adele heard the sound of a motor. Roland stood up and went to a window. "It's a sheriff's vehicle," he said.

Both Adele and Ophelia joined Roland at the window. Adele silently prayed it would be one of Lucas's two deputies exiting the vehicle.

It was Dan Walser. He started walking up to the door with his hand resting on the butt of his gun.

"I take it he is not a friend but a foe," Ophelia said.

Adele's fists clenched at her sides. "You'd be right about that. That's Walser, the man who helped to push Lucas out of a job. According to Yuri, he works for Liya and Visili now."

Ophelia turned around and scurried to the other side of the room. "No worries, God will provide." She returned carrying a shotgun which she then calmly loaded with two shells.

"You two might want to step back a bit. If I have to shoot, there'll be quite a mess."

Both Adele and Roland moved further away from the door with their eyes wide and their mouths hanging open. All three of them waited. A single hard knock echoed inside the room.

"Who is it?" Ophelia yelled out.

Adele heard Walser clearing his throat.

"Dan Walser. I need to speak to Ms. Plank. I have reason to believe she's here with Mr. Soros."

"You have a warrant that requires me to do that, Mr. Walser?" Ophelia yelled back.

"This isn't official business. And as much as Ms. Plank might not believe me, I'm here to try and help Lucas. I didn't sign up for killing anyone and certainly not a cop. I'd like to speak to Mr. Soros as well."

Adele put her finger to her lips to urge Roland to stay quiet while Ophelia responded to Walser. "That's none of your business Mr. Walser. I really think the best course of action is for you to turn around and leave. This is God's home. There is to be no violence here."

"I'm not here to hurt anyone. I told you, I'm here to try and save Sheriff Pine. We don't have much time. Liya and Visili – they're animals!"

Ophelia kept the shotgun pointed at the door. "I believe there's a saying for that kind of thing Mr. Walser - something about lying down with dogs and getting up with fleas."

Walser cursed under his breath. "Will you please let me in? I'm not leaving without talking to Ms. Plank. Here, I'll leave my gun outside."

Roland crept toward the window and then confirmed Walser had put his gun on the ground.

Ophelia looked at Adele. "It's your call."

Adele walked up to the door, gripped the handle, and after a brief moment of hesitation, she opened it.

Walser walked in, realized a shotgun was aimed at him, and froze. "Geez! Put that thing away!"

Ophelia used the gun to point to the table. "Take a seat, Mr. Walser."

Walser quickly did as he was told. He sat down and waited. He was joined by Roland and Adele. Ophelia took a position at the opposite end of the table and remained standing while still holding the shotgun.

"My name is Mother Mary Ophelia. Mr. Soros and Ms. Plank are my guests. I'll allow you to say what you came here to say and then you are to leave, understood?"

Walser nodded. "Understood. Now please stop pointing that gun at me."

Ophelia lowered the shotgun. "Go ahead, Mr. Walser. You have our attention, and we're all waiting to hear what you have to say."

"The first thing you're likely wondering is how I knew you were here Ms. Plank. It was pretty simple actually. Visili called for me to come get him. By the time I arrived, I had a very wet and unhappy Russian on my hands. I literally had to fish him out of the water. Something about a boat chase you two were involved in? Anyways, after I dropped him off safely back onto solid ground, I immediately made my way here. I remembered the framed picture in Mr. Soros's bank. I went there the same day you did. I was following you, actually. I stood outside watching you through a window as you were looking at the picture. After you left, I went in and checked it out for myself. The nun in the picture gave it away. I knew this had to be the place that photograph was taken. Given where Visili's boat went down and the direction you were headed, it didn't take much more to figure out that here is where I would find you both. I was in law enforcement for a long time. This was basic two-and-two stuff."

If Adele's eyes were fists, she would have been pummeling Walser with them. "Well good for you. Now tell me where Lucas is."

"Did Yuri speak to you about the sheriff?" Walser asked.

Adele nodded. "He said if I didn't deliver Roland to Liya and Visili they might kill Lucas. Yuri also made clear that you now work for them."

Walser grimaced. The subject of Liya and Visili clearly made him uncomfortable.

"Those two didn't give me much of a choice. Yuri, for all his faults, was never a cold-blooded killer. He'd rough people up, give them a scare, but killing was never his first move. Liya and Visili? They are more than happy to kill first and ask questions later. They're not the kind of people you can easily to say no to."

Adele could barely tolerate listening to Walser and his excuses. "What about Sergei? Are you going to sit there and tell me Yuri didn't have anything to do with Sergei using Lucas to kill himself? That's what opened the door for you to come in and initiate that sham of an investigation, right?"

Walser's shoulders slumped. "Yeah, that was the plan, but Yuri's hand was forced. Moscow demanded a response for the money that was lost when Mr. Soros pulled the plug on Cattle Point. Yuri had sold the potential of Cattle Point to Moscow big-time. He had them already counting their money. That was his mistake. He was trying to reassert some control over the use of the islands. The sheriff was in the way. Yuri didn't want to kill Lucas. He just wanted him out of the Sheriff's Office. Sergei has nieces and nephews in Vancouver and back in Russia. Yuri promised him his family wouldn't be harmed if he did this one last thing. Sergei was already a marked man because of his part in the Cattle Point fiasco. His time was about up one way or the other. Moscow was gunning for him so he decided to sacrifice himself to save his family so that some good might come from his death."

Ophelia shook her head. "I don't believe Sergei's sacrifice was entirely selfless. It also allowed him to extract some revenge on those he felt put him in the position of having to make that choice in the first place – namely Lucas and Adele who were likely instrumental in Mr. Soros's decision to shut down the Cattle Point project."

Walser shrugged. "Yeah, I suppose so."

"And what is *your* connection to Yuri, Mr. Walser?" Roland asked.

"We did some business years back. I owed him. He told me the plan to have the sheriff investigated and then removed from office. I'm no different than Sergei was. I have family who I care about. I didn't want them hurt, so I agreed. That's it. None of this is terribly complicated."

Adele recalled Denver Wakefield telling her how Yuri had several members of law enforcement on his payroll who helped to get his marijuana shipments across the border. Though Wakefield hadn't confirmed to her that Walser was among those who did so, she had already decided it was the most likely explanation for Walser and Yuri's connection.

"When you were State Patrol you helped Yuri get his marijuana shipments into the state. That was your business with him. You were nothing more than a criminal with a badge."

Walser's face reddened. "None of that matters right now. The only thing you should be thinking about is saving your friend."

As much as Adele despised Walser, she trusted him even less. "And we're supposed to believe that's why you're really here? The same man who cost Lucas his job now wants to help us save him?"

"Yes, but I want assurances that after I do, we're all done with each other. I'll go back to my life away from the islands. I didn't really want any of this, and I certainly don't want people getting hurt."

Ophelia clicked her tongue. "Oh, you poor little thing, all of this mess you helped to create and now you just want your life to go back the way it was? You're attempting to bribe these two in return for helping to save an innocent man! I shudder to think how you have spent most of your adult life being allowed to arrest people at gunpoint."

Walser stood up. "You don't want my help? Fine."

Roland tapped the table with his finger. "Sit down Mr. Walser. I'm not done with you yet."

"*What*? You don't have any authority to tell me what to do."

Roland folded his arms across his chest. "That might be true, but I'm pretty sure the FBI might have a say."

"The FBI? What are you talking about?"

"The same FBI that has been conducting an investigation into Yuri Popov for quite some time. I wonder if they've already made a note of your relationship with him."

Walser's face went white. He slowly lowered himself back into the chair.

Roland smirked. "Good boy. Now, how about you start telling us where we'll find Lucas."

Walser's eyes darted from side to side like a caged rat seeking escape. "I'll tell you, but I want your word that once you get the sheriff back safe, I'm out of this. You, the sheriff, nobody comes after me, OK?"

"But I thought you were running for sheriff yourself Mr. Walser?" Adele mocked. "I saw a sign that said so."

Walser used the back of his hand to wipe perspiration from his brow. "The sign was Yuri's idea. It was meant to help the public see me as their new sheriff. Yuri is always working the angles like that, thinking he's clever."

Roland grunted. "You don't need to tell me how Yuri does business. It's been my misfortune to learn of that first-hand. What I would like to know is who on the council does Yuri have in his pocket? It's become clear someone there has been helping to push his agenda."

Walser shook his head. "I'm no snitch. If you suspect the council that's your problem, not mine. You people are always reminding others how these islands are your home and how you take care of your own. Fine, then deal with your own garbage. Don't ask me to do it for you."

When there was no reply, Walser nearly shouted his frustration. "So do you want me to help you get the sheriff back or not?"

Adele nodded but said nothing. Walser scowled.

"And does that mean we have a deal? After this is finished, I get to leave the islands and be left alone?"

Roland shrugged. "As much control as we might have over such things, yes. You have our word."

Walser pointed at Roland and Adele. "Between your money and her newspaper you two have *plenty* of control. And we all know the both of you have the ear of the sheriff."

A whispered warning sounded in Adele's mind. She had a sense time was running out. Her phone's vibration announced the arrival of a new text. She opened the message and read it.

Please help. They're going to kill us. Come alone. No police or we're dead. Bluff suite @ Rosario. -Vincent

Adele looked up from her phone. Walser stared back at her. She ignored him and turned to Roland.

"We don't need him to tell us. I already know where Lucas is."

Chapter 23

Roland was unusually quiet during the trip over to Rosario. He sat at the back of the Chris Craft on the bench seat looking out at the water, seemingly deep in thought. Next to him was Walser's gun.

At first, Adele had demanded Walser come with them. He refused, saying he was done with the mess Yuri had created. All he wanted was to be left alone. It was Roland who picked up the gun from the ground outside the monastery.

"If you're not coming with us then we need this more than you," he told Walser.

Ophelia urged both Adele and Roland to be careful. As Roland walked ahead toward the road, Adele stayed with Ophelia for a while longer. She remembered something she had wanted to mention to her earlier.

"I knew another Ophelia once. She was born here and was Lucas Pine's girlfriend in high school."

Ophelia nodded. "I know. I read the story you wrote about her. You showed great compassion despite the terrible thing she had done to that poor girl. The fact we share a name is no coincidence. I knew her family well. Her father and brothers were all fishermen. When I was younger, I traveled to Friday Harbor each spring for the blessing of the fleet. That's where I met them. We became friends. Her parents named Ophelia after me. The longer you stay on the islands, the more you'll come to realize how much all of us are connected. When one of us hurts we all share something of that pain. And when there is joy, each of us feels that as well. It is a big part of what makes this place so unique – so human. We deeply care for each other, even those who sometimes do us wrong."

Ophelia hugged Adele.

"I'll pray you end this day safely. I know you're disappointed in Roland and his involvement with Yuri Popov. Remember, though, Roland inherited Yuri from his grandfather at a time when he was far more naïve about such things than he is now. When this is over, I urge you to find forgiveness in your heart for him. He's going to need to know you won't resent him for his past mistakes."

When Adele went to pull away, Ophelia held tightly to her shoulders. "Those who reach my age come to appreciate some undeniable truths regarding life and death. One of those truths is that time is a terminal illness for which there is no cure. It kills us all. Don't waste it holding on to anger against those you love. We all make mistakes, yet we are also redeemable. The young man leaving here with you wants nothing more than to be redeemed in your eyes, Adele. Give him that chance. You never know if it might be the last chance he'll get."

Adele wasn't entirely sure why, but Ophelia's words made her want to cry. She fought back the tears, straightened her shoulders, and nodded.

"Once everyone is safe, I'll work on it. I promise."

Adele's mind returned to the present. She looked up at Rosario's weathered, green-copper rooftops and repeated that same promise to herself. Roland moved to the front of the boat and sat down in the passenger seat next to her. He was holding Walser's gun. His eyes scanned the cliffs that rose up from the water to the resort's massive white stucco walls.

"What's the plan?"

Adele pointed to a small single-story structure located further north from the resort that was perched high above the water. "That's the bluff suite there. We tie up the boat and head on up."

Roland didn't look so certain. "Just like that? You sure we shouldn't let one of Lucas's deputies know what's going on?"

"I already did. Chancee is stationed on Orcas. I texted her before I left Shaw Island. I'm not waiting for her, though. We need to get Lucas back now. Besides, we aren't going there unarmed. I take it you know how to use that thing?"

Roland stuffed the gun into the front pocket of his jacket. "I'd rather not have to, but I'll manage."

Adele held out her hand. "You want me to hold onto it?"

Roland frowned and shook his head. "I said I'll manage."

Once the boat was tied up at the marina, Adele bounded up the steps as Roland followed close behind. She paused at the entrance to the busy resort to look around.

"It feels like we're being watched."

"That's because we probably are," Roland replied.

Adele heard someone giggling behind her. She turned around and found Vincent Weber with his hands covering his mouth. He doubled over and broke out into high-pitched laughter.

"Oh, I'm sorry. I couldn't help it. It's so funny how you both arrived here so serious!"

Adele and Roland shared a confused look. Vincent responded with another bout of giggling. The sound made Adele want to strangle him.

"What is wrong with you? What could possibly be funny about the text you sent? Where's Lucas?"

The question made Vincent laugh even more. He almost toppled over. Adele could smell the alcohol coming off of him. Roland charged forward and grabbed the front of Vincent's shirt.

"Look you little prick we want answers! Who put you up to this? Was it Yuri?"

"No, Mr. Soros. It wasn't Yuri. *I* sent the text."

Adele and Roland turned around. Adele recognized the tall, blonde-haired woman immediately from the Sheriff's Office video footage Samantha had sent her. Liya Vasa was even more intimidating in person. In her heels, she towered over Adele. She stepped toward Roland and caressed his face.

"So, this is Roland Soros, the one who has caused my family such agitation. I did not know you were so pretty. I hope after today we can be friends. Good friends. Of course, business comes first does it not? And that is why we are here."

Liya stared down at Adele. "Ah, the newspaper girl. The trouble-maker. I have no need to be friends with the likes of you. The sheriff, though, you are all he talks about. He threatens he will kill us if we harm you. Over and over he says this. Now I look at you, and I don't understand why. You are so little. So weak. So average in every way."

Adele stared into the eyes of the woman who had killed Avery. Liya pointed toward the lobby.

"Come with me. I have a room waiting. It's private. We can discuss our business there."

Adele glared at Liya. "We're not going anywhere with you until we know Lucas is safe."

Liya's posture stiffened. "Don't think for a second you are in control of this situation newspaper girl. I speak. You listen. I order. You obey. That's how this works. You want to cause problems? Fine. I snap my fingers, and your sheriff loses one of his. Just like that. Don't doubt me and don't test me. Now come. We go."

Vincent wasn't giggling anymore. He looked up at Liya wide-eyed.

"Wait, I don't understand. I thought this was just a prank we were playing. Are you actually threatening these people?"

Liya rolled her eyes. "After you said you don't understand I stopped listening. You bore me. If you want my funding for your film, you will shut up and follow."

Liya walked into the resort. Vincent followed. After a moment's hesitation, Adele and Roland did as well. Roland leaned down and whispered into Adele's ear.

"I'm not a fan of the term, but that woman is a real bitch."

Adele stared at Liya's back. "I was thinking the exact same thing."

Liya led them to a room at the very end of the hall on the second floor. There was no bed, just a circular table and four chairs. The window blinds were shut tight. She ordered everyone to sit at the table and then closed the door behind her.

"OK, this is good. We are all here. I won't waste time."

Liya sat with the others. "Yuri had a profitable relationship with these islands for a very long time but that time has ended. It is now *my* time. Mr. Soros, Yuri borrowed money from my family to invest in your Cattle Point project. Do you know who my father is?"

Roland continued to keep both hands in his pockets. "I've heard of him."

"Good. Then you know he is a powerful man who gets his way. Here I am my father's representative. Yuri owes a debt to him and, given your relationship with Yuri, that debt is also yours. Do you understand?"

Roland shook his head. "No. I paid Yuri's Cattle Point investment back, all of it – every cent. If he didn't use that to pay your father back, that isn't on me. That's between your family and Yuri and it sure as hell doesn't involve my friends. What you're attempting to do here is wrong, and you know it. You, your family, can go to hell. I won't be intimidated."

Liya arched a brow. "Oh, the pretty boy has a bit of spine. I like that. I like it a lot. Now let's see if he has a brain. You'll agree to do business with my family, Mr. Soros. If not, the sheriff will suffer terribly. Here is proof of what I say."

Liya slid her phone across the table. Roland picked it up. When he looked at the screen, Roland's entire body stiffened. He gave the phone to Adele. The image was of Lucas bound, gagged and sitting in a chair. His eyes were closed and his face badly beaten. Adele passed the phone to Vincent who gasped loudly.

"What is happening? Did your brother do that to the sheriff? Why?"

Liya chuckled. "*That*, Mr. Weber, is a message. Now it is up to them to understand what it says."

Vincent pushed away from the table. "I didn't sign up for this. I want nothing to do with it. I'm calling my agent now and getting the first flight out of here."

"Yes, you do that Mr. Weber. And then when you return to Los Angeles one of my family's associates will be there to greet you. No matter where you go, we are already there. Don't believe me? Do what you say, and you will find out soon enough."

Vincent's already high-pitched voice went several octaves higher. "You're threatening me?"

"No, Mr. Weber, I am simply explaining to you how things will work from here on out. I already told you to be quiet. Don't make me have to say it again. I hate when I have to repeat myself. It is so very annoying."

"What does any of this have to do with me?" Roland asked.

Liya smiled. "You owe my family for the money we lost on the Cattle Point project, including interest. All I ask is that you help to finance Mr. Weber's film as partial payment for that debt. It is very simple, yes?"

Roland leaned against the back of his chair. "How much are you hoping to shake me down for?"

"I have already told Mr. Weber I would invest twenty million dollars."

Roland's laughter was a contemptuous bark. "Hah! You're crazy. I don't have that kind of money. I told you – I paid Yuri back everything I owed him which by the way was a lot less than twenty million. I'm tapped out. You're trying to squeeze blood from a stone."

Liya stared at Roland from underneath heavy-lidded eyes. "I think there is *plenty* of blood in you yet."

Again Roland shook his head. "No, there isn't. You're either stupid or terribly misinformed. Besides, if your daddy is so rich and powerful why doesn't he just give you the money to invest in a film? Why do you need me to do it for you?"

Adele watched as Liya's icy exterior suddenly turned hot. She heard the rage in her voice.

"My family's business is not your concern. You refuse my request? Here is another image of the sheriff."

Adele and Roland took Liya's phone. This time it showed Visili standing behind Lucas with a knife digging into the flesh of his throat.

"If we cannot come to an agreement, the next picture will upset you even more. The clock is ticking, Mr. Soros. I can see you sitting there thinking of using the gun in your pocket. If you do, the sheriff dies. His death will be your fault. You don't want that do you? Of course not, it would be so much better for you to give me the gun, so you are not tempted to do something that gets your dear friend killed."

With a growl, Roland took out the gun and pointed it at Liya's face. His breath exited his nose, in short, trembling bursts. Liya shrugged as she glanced at Adele.

"Go ahead. Of course, if you do, you'll not only kill the sheriff but the newspaper girl, too."

Roland's eyes darted from Adele back to Liya. "What?"

"My finger is on the trigger, Mr. Soros. I have a gun under the table. I am pointing it at her right now. You should never allow an enemy to choose the room. I was prepared in case you tried to play tough. But we need not be enemies. No, you and I can be very good friends. It is up to you. Give me the gun. I would hurry. Visili's knife is very sharp, and he is not a patient man."

Roland's hand started to tremble. He muttered a cursed, then lowered the gun and slid it across the table. Liya picked it up with her left hand while keeping her right hand hidden.

"Hmmm, it's heavier than it looks. Much heavier than mine."

Liya moved her right hand out from under the table. The only thing pointing at Adele was her finger. "Bang!" she said with a mocking smile.

Roland went to lunge at the gun. Liya was quicker. She aimed the weapon at Adele.

"No, no, no, Mr. Soros, you don't want to do that. Sit back down. There you go. That is the smart thing. Oh, look at you. Even when you are angry, you are still so pretty! But your time is up. I need an answer now. Do we have a deal? Twenty million dollars for the film?"

Roland slumped in the chair. "I have no idea how I'll come up with that much money, but I'll try."

"You own a bank don't you? I'm sure you'll figure it out. And if not, then you'll just have to work it off another way. There are so many possibilities."

Adele refused to sit and listen to Liya any longer. She stood up.

"OK, Roland agreed. Now, where's Lucas?"

Liya told the two men to remain seated while she stood up as well. She kept the gun aimed at Adele.

"That's right, your sheriff. I almost forgot. You will find him where the text said you would. Take the path at the back of the resort to the top of the hill. He's inside the cabin."

Adele's eyes narrowed. "And that's it? Your brother just lets him go?"

"Well, there is one other thing," Liya replied.

"*What* other thing?" Adele asked.

Liya lowered the gun. "It is up to you and Mr. Soros to make certain the sheriff affords me the same courtesy as previous island sheriffs gave to Yuri. It is expected that where we do business, the sheriff and his department look the other way."

Roland shook his head. "Good luck convincing Lucas of that. You don't know him. He can't be bought and he sure as hell can't be intimidated. I can do my part with raising funds to help finance this film you want to invest in, but as far as the sheriff goes, if it's illegal, he won't go along with anything you have in mind. Not on these islands."

Liya looked Adele up and down. "I'm not so sure of that. You let him know that all those he cares about will be put at great risk should he be anything less than cooperative. No-one will be spared my family's disappointment. You tell him that newspaper girl. He will listen to you, won't he? Yes, I know this to be true. Now go to the cabin on the bluff. Find him there. He is likely to be in some pain but still alive – for now."

Roland stood up so fast the chair fell behind him. "She's not going alone! No way. I'm coming with her."

Liya waved the gun like a finger. "No, you will stay here with me. We will wait. If she tries anything, I kill the director first. Then I kill you."

The color washed out of Vincent's face. "Hey, no, uh, I need to go. I don't belong here."

Liya slammed the butt of the gun into the top of Vincent's skull. The force of the blow sent his face crashing down against the table. Adele heard some of his teeth ricochet off the wood floor. Vincent's body went limp.

"You might have killed him!" Roland cried.

"Keep your voice down, or I *will* kill him," Liya answered. "He's fine. It's just a little bump on the head. Don't be such a baby."

Roland reached down and pressed his fingers against Vincent's neck. He looked back at Adele.

"There's a pulse. He's breathing."

Liya motioned with her gun for Roland to sit. "See? I told you so. Next time, though, I won't go easy on him – or you."

Roland picked up his chair and sat down. Liya turned toward Adele.

"You go to the cabin. Speak to no-one. The sheriff is waiting for you. We are in business now. This will be good. You will see."

Liya opened the door. Adele stepped into the hall. Roland looked at her from across the table with eyes that pleaded for her to be careful.

The door closed.

Adele walked downstairs and into the afternoon sun. She went to the back of the resort where she found the paved path that led up to the guest cabin on the bluff. The path was empty. She jogged up it and then stopped when she came to a clearing. On the other side of that clearing was a small, white, single-story cabin that overlooked the blue-green waters that surrounded Orcas Island.

When Adele saw the cabin something in her wanted to turn away and run. She took several slow, deep breaths. Lucas needed her help. Adele ignored her fear, but it wasn't easy. Mother Mary Ophelia was right; evil had come to the San Juan Islands.

That evil now waited for Adele to come inside.

Chapter 24

Adele's cell phone was dead. She had hoped to find a message from one of Lucas's deputies telling her they were on their way.

No phone.

No message.

She was on her own.

Adele walked toward the cabin. She thought she saw a gap in one of the blinds covering the windows open and then close but wasn't certain of it.

The sound of water licking the rock and pebble beach below was the only sound Adele could hear. The cabin was silent. She hesitated in front of the door wondering if she should knock or just walk in.

The door was flung open. A massive hand reached out, grabbed Adele, and pulled her inside. She was thrown to the floor. The door slammed shut. Lucas was bound and gagged and sitting in a chair against a wall. His eyes flared, and the veins in his neck appeared ready to burst as he struggled to break free.

The back of Visili's hand struck Lucas across his face. "Shut up! We have business to do. You make trouble I will snap her neck like a chicken."

Adele cried out as she was pulled up off the floor by her hair and dropped into a chair on the opposite side of the room. Visili patted the top of her head.

"See, she is fine. You want to keep her that way, be quiet and listen, OK?"

When Lucas nodded droplets of blood from a deep gash on the bridge of his nose fell onto his shoes. Visili nudged Adele's shoulder.

"Tell him you're OK."

Adele looked up. "Lucas, I'm OK. We'll be out of here soon. I promise."

Visili nodded. "Ah, see? This is better. Now I call Liya. We all talk. We do business. Then it is all good."

Visili took out his phone and then stood in front of Lucas. "Now you listen very carefully, Sheriff. Newspaper girl comes here to make a deal, but for the deal to work, we need you to promise you'll what she says. Liya is listening now."

Visili turned and stared down at Adele while holding his phone in front of him. "Go ahead. Tell him how this must work."

Adele folded her hands on her lap and gazed into Lucas's eyes. She hated having to say what she knew she must. Right and wrong were so important to Lucas. He had sworn to protect the islands from scum like Visili. Lucas was already badly hurt, though. She didn't want to see him hurt anymore.

"Lucas, these people will threaten everyone you care about if you don't let them use the islands for their business. They're asking that you look the other way like other sheriffs have done. His sister Liya is holding Roland and Vincent Weber hostage. She promised to kill them both if you don't agree to her demands."

Visili reached down and gripped Adele's chin between his fingers. "And then I'll kill her too, Sheriff. Make up your mind. You are either with us, or you are against us. What is it going to be?"

Lucas hit the wall with his chair and glared at Visili. His eyes burned into the Russian's with such intensity Visili took a half-step back. Adele leaned forward trying to get Lucas's attention.

"We'll make it work, Lucas. Let's get everyone home safe and then we'll find a way to make it work."

Lucas shook his head slowly from side to side while keeping his eyes locked onto Visili's. Adele flinched when she felt a blade pressing against her throat.

"You think I'm playing, Sheriff? Hmmm? You want to see her bleed? It would be so easy. One little flick of the wrist."

Lucas's rage vanished. He no longer shook his head in defiance but compliance. Visili smiled.

"Ah, so you changed your mind? Now you agree to our terms, yes?"

Lucas nodded. When Visili withdrew the knife, Adele heard Lucas let out a grateful sigh. Visili spoke into his phone.

"It is all good. The sheriff has agreed. We have a deal."

Lucas closed his eyes and dropped his head.

"Now let us go," Adele demanded.

Visili's fingers slowly traced the scar on the side of his face. "You and I have business too, don't we? I could have drowned. That wasn't nice. That wasn't nice at all. Now you make it up to me."

Adele began choking when Visili's hand clamped around her neck. She couldn't scream. She could hardly breathe. Visili was too determined and far too strong.

Lucas strained to escape the chair as Visili taunted him. "Why are you upset, Sheriff? I am going to make your friend feel *so good.* You should be quiet so you can hear how much she enjoys it. Yes, you listen and you remember. If you make my sister unhappy with our deal, I come back for the newspaper girl and do it to her again and again and again – just like I do it to her now."

Visili picked Adele up by the throat and hair and dragged her into the adjoining bedroom. He threw her onto the bed, closed the door, and locked it. His grin was malice and his eyes madness. He leaped on top of her and covered her mouth with his hand before she could cry out. She felt his manhood pressing against her thigh. Visili groaned loudly as he adjusted himself over her. He reached down to unzip his pants. Adele opened her mouth as wide as she could and bit down on his hand. When he cursed and tried to pull away, Adele clamped down even harder.

She could taste the bitter copper of his blood as it oozed between her teeth.

"Bitch!" Visili's fist slammed into the side of Adele's head. Her vision detonated into sparkling shards of white and gray.

Don't pass out! Don't pass out!

Visili rolled off the bed, stood up, and staggered backward as he held his bleeding hand out in front of him. "You should not have done that. I was going to go easy on you. Now? Now I hurt you bad. It'll be better for me but not so good for you."

Visili's knife made another appearance. He pointed the blade at Adele.

"Don't move. Don't scream. Just take off your clothes, or I will cut them off you. Either way works for me."

Adele tried to blink away the pounding in her skull. She slid off the bed and stood with her back against the wall. She wanted to sound tough, unafraid, but couldn't. Her voice faltered. Her eyes were wet with tears.

"Don't touch me."

Visili licked his knife. "Oh, I'm gonna do a *lot* more than just touch you. That water you left me in was very, very cold. You owe me."

Adele spread her feet and put up her fists. It was the fighting stance she had learned while studying Taekwondo in college.

"I swear if you come any closer, I'll kill you."

The sound of Visili's deep-throated chuckle made Adele's hands tremble. She knew what was coming next. The blade's metal reflected off Visili's dark eyes.

"Oh, you're so cute! Remember, I *want* you to make some noise. Let your friend in the other room have to sit and listen. The sound will break him just like I am about to break you."

Visili moved forward leering and confident. Adele readied herself to fight. She refused to be an easy victim. Visili lunged to the right with the knife. Adele saw his left hand reach out and knew the knife in his other hand was meant to distract her. She wasn't fooled. Instead, she delivered a hard, snapping punch into the middle of Visili's nose. His head snapped back, and his eyes widened in shock.

Visili shook his head and growled like a deranged beast. The knife descended and plunged hilt-deep into the wall just inches from Adele's face. His other hand encircled her throat. He slammed her head against the wall again and again until she felt her legs buckle.

Adele had tried to fight, but she could fight no more.

Visili's tongue licked her cheek and then her lips. His hand pushed itself inside her shirt and clamped down onto one of her breasts so hard it made Adele cry out. Visili grabbed hold of her jeans and began pulling them down.

The room exploded.

Chapter 25

Lucas hit the door so hard with his shoulder the entire frame broke apart with a thunderous crack. He stood just outside the room with his chest heaving looking wild-eyed at Visili as he lay on top of Adele. Lucas's voice was a seething hiss of volcanic rage that was about to blow.

"Get off her."

Visili rolled away from the bed and stood up. He appeared surprised to see Lucas but not afraid. He pointed to the pieces of the chair Lucas had been tied to that now lay scattered on the floor behind him.

"You broke the chair. I'm not paying for that."

Lucas's hands were still tied. Adele knew that would put him at a terrible disadvantage against the powerfully-built Visili. She got up. Visili snarled for her to get back on the bed.

"Where do you think you're going? I'm not finished with you."

Lucas stepped into the room. "Yes, you are. Adele, get out of here."

Adele hesitated. She didn't want to leave Lucas alone with Visili. Lucas glanced at her. It was just a half-second's distraction. That was all Visili needed.

He charged.

Lucas was thrown backward but he didn't fall. With a snarl, he put his head down and used his shoulder to catapult Visili across the room. The impact against the wall shook the entire cabin. Visili grunted and gasped for breath while Lucas fought to keep the Russian pinned.

Adele searched for anything she might use against Visili. She remembered the knife he had left stuck in the wall. Her eyes scanned the room. She couldn't find it.

The knife was gone.

Lucas gasped. Visili grinned as he pushed Lucas off of him. His dark eyes twinkled at Adele as he pointed to the hilt sticking out from the top of Lucas's blood-soaked shoulder.

"Are you looking for this? Come over here and get it."

Adele stood frozen and mute, terrified and heartbroken. The amount of blood leaking out of the stab wound was too much. Lucas was dying.

Visili stuck out his lower lip. "What's the matter? The little newspaper girl going to cry? I make you cry. I make you cry good and long and loud."

"No!" Lucas bellowed. He stood up straight, rocked his head back, and then sent it crashing into Visili's face. The Russian staggered and almost fell. Lucas turned to Adele with eyes pleading for her to listen.

"Adele, please…RUN!"

Adele took off for the door. She would bring back help and save Lucas.

There was a scream followed by a heavy thud. Adele reached the door and looked back. Lucas was face-down on the floor. Visili stood over him holding the knife. He turned his head slowly and grinned at Adele.

Adele's fingers slipped off the door handle. She let out a panicked wail, grabbed hold with both hands and opened it. Visili's knife cut the air behind her. She stumbled, tried desperately to remain on her feet and then fell onto her hands and knees.

Visili took hold of Adele's hair and turned her over. He leaned down with legs spread, eyes bulging and spit spraying from his mouth.

"No more playing. Game over."

The knife was raised. Adele opened her fingers wide and plunged her hand up into Visili's groin. She hissed through gritted teeth as she grabbed, squeezed, and pulled down – hard.

Visili howled. Adele let go and then used her hands and feet to push herself backward along the ground. When she stood up Visili remained bent over. Sweat covered his face as he took in big gulps of air. Adele looked behind her. She was just a few feet from the cliff-side precipice.

It was a long way down to the rocks and water below.

Adele prepared to run. Visili lurched forward waving the knife in front of him. He blocked the way to the path that led back to Rosario.

"No! You won't get away."

Adele took a step back. Visili crept forward. He licked his lips.

"You're running out of room."

"I'll scream. Somebody will hear me."

"Go ahead. They'll be too late, and then I'll just kill them, too."

Adele opened her mouth. Visili charged. Adele crouched low and rolled to the side. When she looked up, he was teetering on the edge, his eyes wide and his arms flailing. He dropped the knife. Adele heard it clinking against the rocks on its way down.

Visili regained his balance. He glanced behind him at Adele. The grin returned.

"That was close. I lost my knife, but that's OK. I'll just kill you with my hands."

Adele reached down and picked up a stone. Visili started to laugh.

"What? You're going to throw a little rock at---"

Adele's aim was true. The stone struck Visili in the mouth and shut him up. The heel of his shoe slipped a little - just an inch or two.

That was enough.

From where Adele stood it was like slow-motion. Visili's upper body slid back seeming to momentarily separate from his legs. The world went still, a brief pause. Then the legs followed, and the whole of him disappeared.

Adele went to the edge of the cliff. She didn't feel bad about wanting to see the broken body. If anyone deserved to die it was Visili. She looked down.

He wasn't there.

A hand grabbed hold of Adele's ankle and yanked her off her feet. She clawed at the hard earth behind her trying to pull herself away from the edge. The hand held tight. Visili's face popped up from the side of the cliff leering at her.

"Hold still, or we both go down," he hissed.

Adele didn't care. Visili was a dead man. This time she was going to make sure of it. If he took her with him over the cliff then so be it. She pulled back her other foot, the one he wasn't holding, and launched her heel at his head. Every time she felt the bottom of her shoe smack against Visili's skull it was a victory. He begged her to stop. Promised he would let her leave.

Adele kicked and kicked again until the fingers around her leg started to slip away. When Visili tried to use his other hand to pull himself up, Adele slammed her foot on top of it.

Visili roared as he reached out with both hands. Adele roared back. She kicked at his nose, his cheeks and his mouth all while staring into his eyes. It was in those eyes that she found her greatest satisfaction. Visili was about to die. He had underestimated her, and he knew it.

It took just one more kick. Visili was gone.

Adele crawled to the edge and looked down. This time there was a body. The impact of what had happened, what she had done, fully hit her at that moment. She went cold. It was hard to breathe. She stood up. Her legs gave out. She fell to her knees. A canvas of sunlight and water stretched out before her. It was so beautiful. She had never felt so tired.

Adele heard footsteps and voices coming up the trail. She wondered if they were friend or foe. Did it matter? She was too exhausted to care.

Chapter 26

His hand wasn't right. It was too cold. His entire body was too still and quiet – like a corpse. It wasn't Lucas Pine laying there. It wasn't the Lucas Adele knew. She wanted the old Lucas back. The one she was always arguing with, laughing with, and getting into trouble with.

She wanted her friend.

"Hey, there you are," he murmured.

Adele let go of Lucas's hand. He reached out and took hers into his.

"Don't let go. It reminds me I'm still alive."

"Are you cold?" Adele asked.

Lucas's eyes were at half-mast, likely due in part to all the painkillers the medical staff had been giving him. "Yeah, a little bit." He opened his eyes all the way and smiled. "You look good. Everything all right? Did they get Liya?"

Adele would rather not deliver bad news to Lucas while he was still recuperating. She recalled the doctors telling her when he was first admitted just three days earlier that his prognosis was guarded at best. He was in shock after having lost nearly five pints of blood by the time he had arrived via helicopter to the Anacortes trauma center.

When word spread throughout the islands about what had happened to him the line to donate blood stretched around the block. Lucas was still their sheriff. He was respected. More importantly, he was loved.

"C'mon, Adele, spill it. Did Liya get away?"

Adele said yes. She explained how during the chaos that followed Visili's death and the efforts to save Lucas, Liya had somehow managed to slip away from Rosario. Where she escaped to remained a mystery. Most seemed to think it was back to Russia. Others believed she was hiding out in Vancouver. Some even said Belize. It didn't really matter at this point. Liya was gone – for now.

Lucas gave a weak shrug. "At least we can say good riddance to her brother. Speaking of which, how are you doing? You OK about what happened?"

Adele lowered her head. She was tired of talking about it. People called her a hero, said she was brave, a survivor. She didn't feel like any of those things. Once the adrenaline was gone, once Lucas was safely in the hospital, she was left with the image of Visili falling. The sound it made - the finality of it. Sure, she had no choice. Adele kept telling herself that as did everyone else. And yet, it still bothered her. She couldn't shake the feeling that she had done something outside of herself. That kicking Visili off the cliff was an act carried out by someone else – a dangerous stranger who lived inside of her. It was someone angry, violent, and deadly. Adele prayed she would never have to meet that stranger again.

"You don't forget, but it *will* get easier," Lucas whispered.

Adele looked up. "Do you still think about what happened that day with Sergei?"

Lucas closed his eyes. "I do. You tell yourself you had no choice, but there's this little sliver of guilt stuck somewhere down deep that you can't pick out that makes you wonder if it isn't really true. You think maybe it's just you making excuses because you don't want to consider the alternative. I know this for sure. I never want to have to pull my weapon on someone ever again."

There was something in how Lucas said those words that Adele didn't like. "What do you mean?"

Lucas opened his eyes and stared up at the ceiling. "Since I woke up here I've done a lot of thinking. Maybe I'm not cut out for being sheriff. Maybe it's time I do something else."

"Stop talking like that. You saved my life, Lucas. Nobody else could have done what you did in that cabin. The way you fought, how you didn't give up, it was amazing. I owe you…"

Adele's voice cut out as she fought back tears. She sniffled, sat up in her chair, and squeezed Lucas's hand.

"I wouldn't be here if it wasn't for you. You feel bad for what happened with Sergei because you're a good man. You're exactly the kind of sheriff we need, and it's exactly the kind of friend I want. Please, give yourself more time to get back on your feet before you make any serious decisions. The doctors say the operation on your shoulder went well. There shouldn't be any long-term complications. You're going to be as good as new. I just know it."

Lucas pushed his head back against the pillow. "Yeah, I suppose you're right. You seem to be right about a lot of things these days. It's actually kind of infuriating."

Adele laughed. A bit of the old Lucas was returning. They spent the next thirty minutes talking. She told him about the memorial for Avery that took place earlier that day. He said he was sorry he couldn't be there and asked how Bess was doing. Adele assured him Bess was doing fine. She had been amazed by the number of people who had come to pay their respects, telling Adele she would never have imagined how so many would care so much.

When Adele mentioned how Decklan and Calista Stone had officially decided to pull the plug on the film adaptation of their story, and that Vincent Weber had already made a hasty retreat back to Hollywood, Lucas nodded. He thought that was probably for the best. Adele agreed. They were both pleased to see him gone from the islands.

Then the subject of Roland came up. Adele knew it would. Roland had been the first to reach her after she had kicked Visili off the cliff. He had been to the hospital to see Lucas just once right after the operation when Lucas wasn't yet awake. Roland left soon after. Adele hadn't spoken to him since. She wondered if he was retreating a bit out of guilt for what had happened. Lucas shook his head and said whatever guilt Roland might be feeling would be short-lived. That he had always been an in-the-moment kind of guy. Adele wasn't so sure. She saw something in Roland's eyes that told her a change had taken place.

Lucas snickered. Adele asked him what was so funny.

"Ever since you showed up to these islands, I've been getting my ass kicked. This last time, though, man what a doozy! It sure seems like you and trouble hang out a lot together."

Adele knew Lucas was right and she felt terrible about it. She did have a knack for finding trouble and trouble finding her.

"I'm so sorry. I guess it's my job, or maybe it's just something about me that attracts…"

Lucas interrupted. Now he was the one who was sorry.

"I didn't mean to make you feel bad. It just struck me as funny is all. These adventures of yours that I end up getting dragged into, to tell you the truth I wouldn't have it any other way. Nobody can ever say being friends with Adele Plank is boring."

Adele squeezed Lucas's hand. "You sure you don't mind all the mess I've dropped on your plate in just the last couple of years we've known each other?"

Lucas squeezed back. "I don't mind. Not even a little."

Adele left the hospital feeling far better than when she had arrived. Lucas was getting stronger. He would be discharged by the end of the week. The San Juan Islands summer season was in full bloom. Life was again returning to normal, and that meant she had a story to tell.

Chapter 27

The Island Gazette

Rosario's Revenge
by Adele Plank

A new friend recently told me that evil had come to the San Juan Islands. She was right. Visili Vasa was an evil man who did terrible things. In this digital age, news on the islands spreads fast. The confrontation Sheriff Lucas Pine and I had with Mr. Vasa was no different. Most of you reading this now have likely already heard some version of the events that took place last week.

Mark Twain, upon being told he had died, famously replied to the world that reports of his death had been greatly exaggerated. I don't mean to place myself next to someone of Twain's stature, but I will say this: I'm here, and for the most part, I'm doing OK.

The same can be said for Sheriff Pine. He survived a terrible attack and very much remains among the living. I am certain all members of the County Council will act swiftly to reinstate him as our sheriff. This community needs him now more than ever. The recent investigation leveled against him after the shooting death of Sergei Kozlov was bogus from beginning to end. The man who oversaw that investigation has since fled the islands in disgrace. The council members who supported Mr. Walser are complicit in this wrongdoing. At the very least, they should be ashamed. That isn't enough, though. Justice demands more. It is my hope that soon they will be voted out of office by the people of these islands who rightly demand fair and honest governance.

Mr. Vasa's sister Liya remains at large. I'm certain she will read this column. In fact, I hope she does. Ms. Vasa, I'm here and should you return to these islands, I'll be waiting. We *all* will. Those who love this place, from the southern tip of Lopez to the northern border points of Patos, are especially determined and resilient people. Visili Vasa learned that firsthand. Unfortunately for him, he learned it too late.

Yes, evil did come to our islands. It infected our streets, darkened our politics, troubled our friends and colleagues, and threatened our lives. Yet on the cliffs overlooking Rosario, that evil came to an abrupt and deserved end.

Rosario had its revenge.

Epilogue

"I do the same thing, you know. The difference is you read yourself, and I watch myself, but I'm sure you get the idea. Guess that means you and me have something in common."

Adele put down her copy of *The Island Gazette* to look up at Action Five News reporter Marianne Rocha. "What do you want? I'm busy."

"Really? Since when is lounging in a lawn chair next to a sailboat while catching some rays considered busy?"

"I see you showed up overdressed again. High heels on the boat dock are a particularly nice touch. Well done."

Marianna adjusted her skirt and flashed her TV-ready smile. "You don't like me much do you?"

"No, I don't. I'll ask you one more time. What do you want? You're a long ways from Seattle. People come to a place like this to get away from people like you."

"Well, aren't you all kinds of nice this afternoon, Ms. Plank? I'm here for a couple reasons, actually. One, I like it. I plan on visiting more often. Second, I have a proposition for you."

Adele stretched her sun-kissed legs out in front of her, put her hands behind her head, and leaned back in the chair. "You don't say? Let's hear it."

"There's still a story going on in these islands. You would know that better than anyone. I have no problem admitting to you that my original reporting was off base. Walser was feeding me false information meant to hurt the sheriff, and I apologize for that. I'm hoping we can put that behind us and work together. I'm willing to share credit with you for any reports I go on air with."

"Uh-huh. And why would I want to do that? I don't care about having my name dropped on your local news broadcast."

"I can help with your investigations. I have good sources outside of the islands. For example, did you know the Feds took Walser in earlier for questioning this week?"

Adele nodded. "Yeah, Sheriff Pine already told me."

"Well, did you also know Walser was released less than an hour later and that the man heading the investigation, an agent named Randall Eaton, has officially classified Walser as merely a person of interest?"

Adele sat up. "Who told you that?"

"Like I said, I have good sources. And I believe this thing goes beyond just Walser. It goes beyond your county council that I suspect has at least one person on there who was working with Walser against the sheriff. Think about it. Who benefitted the most from what happened to Liya and Visili Vasa? Liya is somewhere in hiding. Visili, as you well know, is dead. Who does that leave as the last man standing in Vancouver as far as Moscow is concerned?"

Adele's jaw clenched. "Yuri Popov."

Marianne nodded. "That's right. Yuri was being put out to pasture and then suddenly Liya is gone, and Visili is eliminated, and Yuri can say he had nothing to do with it. His hands are clean. Moscow has no choice, at least for now, to have him continue as the man running its Vancouver operations."

"You're telling me Yuri had Lucas and me do his power struggle dirty work for him?"

"It looks that way. Don't feel bad. Yuri Popov is a survivor and a sneaky one at that. There aren't a lot of old men with his kind of resume. Most die or end up in prison. Not him. He's managed to avoid both up to this point. This wasn't his first rodeo. There were two likely outcomes in Rosario, right? Either you and the sheriff took out Visili and Liya, or they took you out. If it had been Liya and Visili, the Feds would be after them for murder right now, and Yuri remains running Vancouver. If they lose, which they did, Yuri *still* remains running Vancouver. He had both sides covered. It was a game where regardless of the outcome he came out the winner."

"I feel pretty stupid," Adele said.

"Don't. I told you, Yuri Popov is as slippery as they come. All the research I've done points to the islands having been used as his halfway point between Vancouver and Seattle for a very long time. I'm guessing you've already done some of that same research. I know detectives who spent entire careers trying to take Popov down. You've already come closer to doing that than anyone. That's why we really should work together. Don't think for a second Yuri is done with you. Remember, Visili was Vlad Vasa's son. I'm certain Vlad has already made it very clear to Yuri that won't be allowed to go unpunished. As sneaky as Yuri is, Vlad is many times more ruthless and powerful. We need to get them before they get you."

"I need some time to think about it."

Marianne nodded. "I understand. We didn't exactly get off on the right foot, did we? We would make a good team, though. I'm not just a pretty face. I'll be in touch. Until then keep enjoying this sunshine."

The two women shook hands. Marianne turned to leave and then stopped.

"Oh! Happy birthday!"

"How did you know it was my birthday?"

Marianne smiled. "Roland Soros told me. I spoke to him earlier. He really is a fascinating man, isn't he? And not at all bad on the eyes. I'm considering doing a full interview with him - sort of an 'island mogul' thing. Hey, speak of the devil, that looks like him heading this way now. You take care, Ms. Plank. I look forward to us working together."

When Roland and Marianne passed each other on the dock, Roland smiled and nodded. Marianne gave a little wave while she tossed her hair over her shoulder and then looked back at him as he made his way toward Adele. He was carrying a large pink box.

"There's the birthday girl. I bet you thought I forgot. Not a chance. Here, I had this made up especially for you."

Adele opened the box and found a beautifully intricate cake inside. She was about to say thank you when she heard more footsteps. She leaned to the side to look past Roland and saw Lucas coming toward her. He was still recovering from his shoulder surgery. One arm was in a sling. His free hand held a little cupcake with a single candle in the center. Roland glanced down at the cupcake and chuckled.

"Something funny?" Lucas asked.

Roland put his arm around Adele and grinned. "I was just noticing how much smaller yours is compared to mine. There's hardly a mouthful there."

Adele poked Roland's side with her elbow. "Real classy, now stop it. I like them both. I actually did think everyone forgot. Not that it's a big deal. I've never been much for my own birthdays anyways."

The cake and cupcake were set down on the bow of Adele's sailboat. Lucas cleared his throat and then used his thumb to point behind him.

"I brought along something else."

It was a happy collection of familiar faces from the islands who Adele had come to know and love. Tilda was at the front with Bess Jenkins. Behind them were Decklan and Calista Stone followed by Suze and Samantha and others. Tilda stopped and smiled and spread her arms wide.

"On behalf of everyone here, I would like to wish a very happy birthday to our Adele. I'm also inviting you all to a celebration in Adele's honor at the hotel this evening. For now, though, there's just one more thing. We sing!"

It wasn't the most melodic rendition of the Happy Birthday song, but the sentiment was beautiful – and appreciated. Adele said thank you over and over as people stepped forward to give her a hug. Tilda was among the last to leave. She squeezed Adele's shoulders.

"I'll see you tonight? No dropping everything to run off on another adventure, OK? You're my guest of honor. That would be rude."

"Of course I'll be there, Tilda. Thank you."

With Tilda gone, only Roland and Lucas remained. Roland leaned down and kissed Adele's forehead and then whispered into her ear.

"Happy birthday, sexy."

Lucas waited for Roland to start walking away before he came up to Adele. He didn't say anything at first. With his one good arm, he pulled her close and held her against his chest. When Adele started to pull away, he held her even more tightly.

"Back in Rosario, when Visili took you into that room and shut that door…I thought I was going to lose you. I couldn't let that happen. No matter what, I just couldn't."

Lucas rested his cheek against Adele's head. "If you don't mind, I'd like to keep holding you like this for a while longer."

Adele didn't mind. Not even a little.

COMING IN 2018:
Book #5 of the San Juan Islands Mystery series:

Roche Harbor Rogue

The entire San Juan Islands Mystery series in order:

*******The Writer*
*******Dark Waters*
*******Murder on Matia*
*******Rosario's Revenge*
*******Roche Harbor Rogue* – coming soon!

About The Author

D.W. Ulsterman is the writer of the Kindle Scout-winning *San Juan Islands Mystery* series published by Kindle Press as well as the bestselling, *The Irish Cowboy.*

He lives with his wife of twenty-five years in the Pacific Northwest. During the summer months, you can find him navigating the waters of his beloved San Juan Islands. He is the father of two children who are now both attending university and is also best friends with Dublin the Dobe.

Made in the USA
Coppell, TX
05 May 2022

77464608R00167